Cheraser's Journey

Cheraser's Journey

Paul Dakin

p.dakin2@ntlworld.com

ISBN 978-1-4477-4423-8

To Debs, Josh and Ellie.

There must be a creator with a loving heart.

To my family.

Thanks for your walking example of love and truth.

Contents

Introduction

Cheraser loves to have fun, and he lives for the moment. His long-term future plans just about stretch to the following weekend. He likes an easy life and tries to avoid all stressful situations – such as getting out of bed before lunchtime.

He is a normal guy, doing normal things that young people do. He isn't particularly unhappy, but he can only hold on to a feeling of well-being fleetingly, and he has an underlying sense of dissatisfaction with his life.

As he begins a journey to discover a deeper reason for his existence, Cheraser tries to find something which will quieten the voice of emptiness that often calls out to his conscience. There is a void in his inner being and this unoccupied space resembles an empty locked box that moves around uncomfortably within him.

Cheraser uses pleasure-seeking activities and spiritual experiences as keys to try to unlock the box and fill it with meaning and lasting satisfaction. However, whatever he uses as a key will not open the box, and unknown to him, no amount of effort will ever find a key which will fit the lock.

Cheraser is searching for peace and freedom, but it seems that all he can find is addiction and increasing dissatisfaction.

Maybe there isn't a deeper meaning to his existence and his search will eventually prove to be futile. But something niggles at Cheraser. Surely there is more to life than what he is experiencing at the moment.

Will he continue to use the same old keys, in a pointless attempt to unlock the box, or will he consider the possibility that there is someone who can unlock the box for him?

If absolute truth is a reality, there must be other people who know about it. Will they engage with genuine spiritual seekers like Cheraser?

Cheraser had started a journey. It would be a battle to find the truth.

1.

Spiritual Awakening

Cheraser leant over the plastic table outside the front of the pub to retrieve his beer bottle from amongst the large hoard already collected there. This kind of table always seemed to have one leg shorter than the rest – whichever way it was moved or turned, or even if one leg was propped up with a piece of cardboard, it still seemed unstable. This one was no different.

As Cheraser gently advanced a steady hand towards his drink, the inevitable happened. With a crescendo of noise, a domino effect of bottle on bottle saw most of the empties rolling around on the table. Luckily, the bottles with some liquid refreshment still inside were saved by some quick reactions. Nonetheless, a couple of recently washed and ironed shirts caught a few splashes. The sound of ironic cheering arose immediately, but Cheraser didn't react apart from a wry smile as he leant back in his seat.

Cheraser enjoyed drinking, but the pub itself was a big part of his life. There was a great sense of community, and Cheraser felt that he belonged here. It was a place of escape, with no strings attached. He used every spare moment as a pleasure-seeking opportunity, even if the feeling of happiness and satisfaction lasted for only a short time. He enjoyed life, but recently he had become frustrated with the number of choices he had.

When the laughter died down, Cheraser and his mates sat outside the pub in silence. Although there was no conversation at the moment, it was the comfortable quiet that you can only experience when you are with a group of people who you know quite well.

The group sat looking out onto a busy town centre. A couple walked past hand in hand, both with garish hair in contrast with their black clothes. Then a woman who seemed to have one leg longer than the other hobbled by awkwardly. She was followed by a man holding a large Bible and rambling about the need to repent before the end of the world.

Some of his friends saw this people watching as an opportunity to laugh at others, but Cheraser was fascinated. This human zoo he was staring at seemed to be symbolic of his own life. There was no particular direction in the way in which some people moved around the town centre, but there were plenty of distractions along the way to keep them occupied.

Cheraser chose music, sport, drinking and nightclubs as his distractions, so that he didn't need to think too much. They were fun but when they ended he was often left with a feeling of emptiness. He pondered on these things and his life suddenly seemed to be so shallow. It was enjoyable, but with no real purpose.

> Cheraser let himself slip into a daydream. He envisioned a large wooden cross, the type of cross used for crucifixion. There was a door built into the bottom of this cross, and there was a heavy chain locked tightly around it. As he stared at the cross, Cheraser longed to know what mystery and adventure lay just beyond the locked door.
>
> Cheraser realised that things had changed for him. He was intensely aware of an indescribable but nonetheless real void within him. Surely there was more to life than this packaged, structured world, where it seemed there had to be a rational answer for almost everything. He was determined to discover what the true mystery of life was all about.
>
> Cheraser looked around and saw that the cross was situated at the side of a wide pathway, which was dry, dusty and well trodden.
>
> He had taken only a couple of steps on the path when a man appeared beside him and attempted to persuade Cheraser to leave the path, using a forceful and confident manner. The man had a very smart appearance and friendly character, but he was quite pushy.
>
> 'A lot of people have tried to walk this pathway before, but it is a waste of time. You only live once – enjoy yourself while you're alive,' he said, very convincingly. 'You need to get back to a more comfortable place,' he added. His words seemed to carry a genuinely caring tone.
>
> Cheraser didn't question the man's comments and decided he wanted to leave the pathway immediately.

'Move to the edge of the path and enter the doorway at the base of the wooden cross,' the man said, firstly pointing the way, and then gently pushing Cheraser towards it. The man unlocked the chain that was wrapped around the door and opened it, and Cheraser walked through, feeling a sense of bewilderment.

'You've been a while in that toilet. Are you trying to avoid your round?' said a friend, as Cheraser returned to his seat outside the pub. This, of course, led them to discuss the best way to avoid paying for a drink. First was the obvious idea of making sure you are the last person into the pub behind your mates – at least one person will either be a generous type or be embarrassed into buying you one. Then, when you are getting towards the end of your first drink, you should perhaps leave an amount in the bottom of your glass, just enough for everyone to see. This will make it obvious that you are not yet ready for another drink, and therefore, there is no need to buy yet. Then hopefully someone else will ask you if you want one. Or perhaps you will soon be moving to another pub. You could then drink up, and again be the last person into the next venue. At this point a couple of lads at the table looked down nervously at the floor. Maybe they would buy the next round of drinks.

It was now early evening, and Cheraser and his friends headed inside the pub to watch the live football that was about to start. At least it was another ninety minutes of escape from reality. The match passed quickly, and afterwards it was a game of pool, something to eat, a few more drinks, and then onto a nightclub. Anything that extended the night was a good thing, and Cheraser, fuelled by alcohol, was buzzing. This is what life is all about, he thought to himself.

As Cheraser awoke early the next afternoon he felt that familiar feeling of loneliness. The buzz he had been feeling only hours earlier had been snatched away by his own body in the process of repairing itself, and replaced with a sense of emptiness. As he lay in bed he was surrounded by the stale aroma of alcohol and aftershave; it always welcomed him back to reality on the day following a night out. Cheraser stared at the ceiling.

As Cheraser started to tread the dusty track once more, he was immediately joined by a group of men and women. They all seemed to be similar in character to the first man he had met on the path, friendly again, but quite controlling. They gathered around Cheraser, bombarding him with

> promises of escaping the feeling of loneliness that they seemed to know he felt.
>
> 'All you have to do is leave the path and turn your computer on,' said one of the men.
>
> 'No one will see you if you shut the curtains. You know it will fill the emptiness for a while,' said another.
>
> There was a sudden silence as a lone female raised her hand. She had a veil over her face, but it didn't hide her amazing beauty. Her brown eyes were almost hypnotic as they sparkled below her dark eyelashes, and she tilted her head to one side as she swept her hands through her long black hair. She took Cheraser by the hand and gently introduced herself.
>
> 'Hi, my name is Stul,' she said. She was mysterious and powerful, and there was no need for her to say anything else. She gently took hold of Cheraser's hand and walked with him to the edge of the path, towards a cross. She unlocked a chain around a beautifully carved door at the bottom of it and pushed the door open. Cheraser felt compelled to walk through it, and he did so willingly.

Cheraser got out of bed and turned his computer on. He told himself that he was just going to read some emails, or talk to some friends online, but he knew that would not last long. The adrenaline soon kicked in, and he was completely focused on the screen. Pornography was another escape for him, and the computer was an easy way to access that kind of material.

There was no need for an embarrassing visit to a newsagent where you pretended to look at a television magazine for ten minutes before eventually standing on tiptoe to grab what you really came for, or the long wait at the counter as the shop assistant took an eternity to locate the price on the front cover. Even if the elusive price was discovered before the queue behind formed into a human conga, you would probably drop your carefully arranged correct change into the narrow gap between the charity collection box and the pile of newspapers, causing more delay in getting away from the shop.

Cheraser had never felt comfortable buying in this way. Online felt much more private, and a lot of the material was free. It seemed like a safe place to be, and these women were his friends. Although they were real people, he wasn't aware of their personalities or, rather, the humanness within their personalities. In other words, he didn't have to live with their faults. It was a virtual relationship and, in some ways, just like the short-term ones he had in real life. There was no commitment and no sense of responsibility. It was a purely self-centred connection, although it did provide a feeling of intimacy.

He thought at first that looking at pornography would get it out of his system, but, in fact, the opposite happened: however much he viewed, it was never enough. Sometimes, hours passed by so quickly in the cyber fantasy world, but it filled the emptiness within, if only for a short time. The problem was that afterwards the loneliness he felt was even more intense. This created a cycle of needing to look at more and more to fill the emptiness, which in turn created more loneliness.

As Cheraser came away from his computer, his mind was in a dizzy haze, as it often was after being online. He got into a warm bath and was comforted by the soft bubbles. His senses were slightly dulled, and he really didn't feel like being around anyone else.

He had these feelings occasionally, which left him quite apathetic. He felt like a prisoner within himself, chained to a mixture of boredom, frustration, and lack of purpose in his life. He knew that these feelings could be released, if only temporarily, by moving on to another new experience or activity, and his attention was drawn to a leaflet he had recently left on the bathroom floor.

> Cheraser sat passively on the pathway. This time he was alone, and he needed someone or somcthing to bring life and excitement to the barren, empty track. Soon, he became aware of a couple of men drawing alongside him. They seemed to have an aura of power and excitement. This time, Cheraser was first to initiate the conversation. He enquired what the men were doing on the pathway, and they were only too pleased to tell him.
>
> 'My name is Lutocc. I can tell you how to experience power and freedom,' said the first man, who was taller and more talkative than the other. 'Your feelings of emptiness will disappear. You can experience whatever you want if you are willing to put in the effort. More importantly, you can be completely in control of what you do,' he added.

> Cheraser was interested in anything that could bring meaning into his life. 'This sounds exactly like what I am looking for. Please share this information with me.'
>
> Without a word, the second man smiled, touched Cheraser on the shoulder, and pointed to the edge of the path. There at the edge was a cross, dark in colour, with a magnetic emotional pull. Lutocc unlocked the chain around the door at the base of it, and Cheraser hurried through.

Cheraser reached out of the bath to pick up the leaflet. It was an advertisement for a psychic evening that was to be held at a local pub. He always found it a challenge to read anything in the bath without ruining it, and this occasion was no different. After finding the date and venue of the event, he placed the leaflet on the bathroom floor to dry before its untimely disintegration.

Cheraser decided that he would attend the psychic night that was to take place in a couple of days. He never took things like horoscopes seriously, but he was intrigued by the mystery of fortune-telling, mediums and hypnotism.

He was now losing valuable time at the pub, and he quickly got out of the bath, dressed, and headed towards his favourite licensed establishment. On the way, he thought about the possibility of the existence of something supernatural.

When Cheraser arrived at the pub, most of his mates were heavily into a discussion about the previous day's football results. At the first opportunity, he mentioned the psychic night, and this started a long debate about the mysteries of life. Was there a possibility that a supreme God-like being existed? Were ghosts, UFOs, and aliens a reality? Was death the end of any kind of conscious awareness?

Of course, there were lots of different opinions. Some people were cynical and stated that they believed everything that was, supposedly, supernatural had rational explanations. They argued that people's beliefs, sightings, and experiences were coincidences, natural occurrences made into something else by human imagination, or frauds by people who wanted to make money from them or who just wanted the attention of having a story to tell. And then there were some who did think there was the possibility of another dimension to life, but they had no idea what that was.

A few of Cheraser's friends decided that they would like to accompany him to the psychic night. They hoped it would provide some kind of spiritual experience. Cheraser didn't know whether they were really intrigued or if they just wanted to go for a good laugh, but the conversation had provoked a lot of thought. He felt a sense of excitement as he looked forward to the event.

After what seemed to be a long, boring couple of days, the evening of the psychic night finally arrived. Cheraser hoped it would add some meaning to his life, but he didn't know whether he was expecting too much. He was almost hyperactive with anticipation because he knew that the world would be a positive place for him to live in for a short time. But he also knew that as soon as the night out ended, the next morning would inevitably bring with it a cloak of low feelings, which wrapped itself tightly around him.

The moment was all that mattered, though, so, at this time, his mood was good. Cheraser didn't have a high opinion of his own appearance; therefore, it took him ages to get ready to go anywhere. He was still touching and prodding his hair twenty minutes after it was dry. He rarely thought he looked just right and overcompensated with a bit too much hair gel and a splash more aftershave than was required. His skin was prone to the odd outbreak of spots, and even one new, tiny blemish could remove all his confidence for days. He often stared at three or four different mirrors in different areas of his house for ages, and, in his own mind, a spot could treble in size in minutes.

At last, he was ready to go, and he took the short walk to the pub. The adrenaline pumped his already good mood into a natural heightened state of well-being. He wished that he could bottle this feeling, but he knew that it was only a fleeting moment that would be stolen from him during the next night's sleep.

He met up with some mates at the pub. They didn't get to the bar without first handing over some money to the gambling machine. The allure of the flashing lights was always too much to resist and normally resulted in everyone having less money by the time they eventually did get a drink, and tonight was no different. An early big win for Cheraser soon became a loss, as the next big win was always just one more spin away. There was less time spent on the gambler tonight, though, as a larger than usual crowd had turned up for the psychic evening.

Cheraser and his mates bought some drinks and settled into some comfortable seats, ready for a night of entertainment. The atmosphere was good, and the pub was filled with chat and the sound of clinking glass. The talk in the pub, as always in a large group of people, was indecipherable, but slowly the noise decreased and turned into a quiet anticipation as everyone waited for the evening to begin.

A hypnotist took to the floor first, and two volunteers were quickly chosen. With a suggestion from the hypnotist and a click of his fingers, both sat with their heads down and eyes shut within seconds, apparently asleep. The volunteers were then told that they were going to be doing certain activities. The first was told she was driving a car, and the second was told he was talking to a mate on the telephone. When the hypnotist clicked his fingers again, the pub erupted into laughter as both of the volunteers acted out their respective roles. With another click and a suggestion from the hypnotist that they would wake up and remember nothing, both 'victims' awoke and, looking slightly perplexed, went back to their seats. Other volunteers were then brought forward to act out roles which ranged from the mundane to the bizarre. This provoked some thought from Cheraser.

> Cheraser was quickly joined by a familiar face.
>
> 'Do you have some questions?' asked Lutocc.
>
> 'Yes,' replied Cheraser. 'Were they all pretending, and is this healthy?'
>
> 'Some were putting it on a bit, but others were hypnotised,' said Lutocc. 'It's the power of suggestion. It's all good harmless fun though, so relax and enjoy the night. There's going to be a lot more entertainment, and there is real power in some of this stuff,' added Lutocc convincingly.
>
> Cheraser didn't have to be persuaded to leave the pathway. There was a cross nearby, and he stepped quickly through the door at the bottom of it. As he did so, he received a gentle pat on the back from someone holding a key who had obviously just unlocked the chains that now hung loose.

He was snapped out of his thoughts by applause for the hypnotist as his act came to an end. Cheraser was now really starting to get into the night, and he wanted to experience more of this. There were some workshops involving palm reading, tarot cards, and meditation, and he needed no encouragement to participate. He was flattered when the palm reader said Cheraser would enjoy good fortune in the near future, and the tarot cards indicated something similar. Cherasers's mates watched, and immediately afterwards one of them offered to buy him a drink. This brought howls of laughter, as it seemed that his friend was trying to guarantee a share in his imminent lottery win.

Cheraser was captivated most of all, though, by a meditation and self-improvement workshop. It was all about the power of positive thinking and finding inner peace. He found this concept very appealing and decided to buy some books about the subject that had been made available for purchase. He really wanted to learn more, and maybe this was the way to find true happiness.

To end the night, a spiritualist medium tried to contact the dead, but alcohol had had plenty of time to take effect, and the poor man was the victim of some serious heckling.

'Someone here has a dead relative with a name beginning with *S*,' shouted one slightly inebriated punter.

'Yeah, and it's either a male or a female,' came another drink-fuelled reply.

Cheraser enjoyed the banter, but he was also slightly disappointed, as he had wanted to see the guy in action. But the moment had been lost, and there didn't seem to be a way back for the flustered medium as his show died.

Cheraser had seen enough. As he walked home, he was glad he wasn't sleeping in the pub overnight. It was weird how he had found the evening interesting, almost compelling, but at the same time he left feeling quite fearful. There was plenty to think about, though, and Cheraser hurried home to look at the books that offered hope of a happy future.

He didn't read books that often, mostly just magazines, but if he did have a new book, he often opened it up and read bits around the middle or the end in the hope of finding something interesting, anywhere other than the start.

When Cheraser got in from a night out, he often turned the television on and channel hopped. Maybe he would catch some action from a late night film or see the free view from a satellite porn channel. He always regretted it in the morning when he was sleep deprived, but, at the time, anything to extend the evening was a good thing. Tonight was different, though, and he went straight to bed, flicking through his new books.

He read and re-read the pages. The words weren't registering in his brain, and his head kept lurching forward as if it was angrily trying to waken him from the early stages of sleep. Cheraser decided it would be better to leave his new reading material for a time when he was less tired, and he dropped the books gently onto the floor.

He stretched out under the duvet and quickly realised how cold the bed was, apart from the exact place where he had been lying for the previous few minutes. He returned to that position and then entered the time between waking and sleeping where thoughts rampage through the mind, sometimes in an irrational manner.

> Cheraser stood on the pathway with his head down. He was soon joined by Lutocc and his companion.
>
> 'Make sure you read those books,' said Lutocc. 'Remember, they will help you to have power and lead you to happiness if you study them diligently. This is a training time. I will lead you to many supernatural experiences if you have an open mind. There is also loads of stuff on the Internet as well, so make sure you have a look.'

At around 2.00 a.m., Cheraser awoke and felt quite fearful. As he looked around his bedroom, there appeared to be a shadow over his wardrobe door. He quickly turned a light on which revealed nothing more threatening than the shirt he had hung there only a few hours earlier. He eventually drifted back to sleep. When he awoke and was greeted by the light of a new day, all his feelings of fear had disappeared.

Cheraser went straight onto the Internet, and typed the word 'meditation' on a search engine. He found material much easier to read on his computer than from a book, even when the words were the same. He had previously thought meditation involved sad people with glazed eyes who filled sports halls with their strange antics. But as he browsed through more and more Web pages, he realised that it offered a way of gaining a spiritual experience. The pages offered advice that could lead to improved mental and physical health and a general feeling of well-being.

Cheraser did not see himself joining any kind of meditation or self-improvement class. He had seen too many weird people sitting in funny positions or walking slowly while making strange hand movements that resembled karate in slow motion. But he could meditate at home, without having to meet or talk to anyone else. It was completely individualistic. Whatever he was looking for, and he wasn't quite sure what that was yet, he thought he could find within himself.

Meditation seemed to be a good place to start, so he decided to try breathing exercises and repeating a phrase over and over again to calm and empty his mind.

> The pathway was now clothed in a blanket of fog. Cheraser hadn't been able to see very far ahead on previous occasions, but now he could hardly see at all. Almost immediately, there was a voice that provided him with some comfort.
>
> 'Well done,' said Lutocc. 'You like the feelings within yourself, don't you? But you need my help to get to the next stage.'
>
> The fog lifted slightly, and Cheraser felt a closer friendship with Lutocc. As they talked, Lutocc moved him towards the door of another cross. After unlocking the chain around it, Lutocc helped him through.

Cheraser liked what he was getting into, but he needed more. He wasn't satisfied with the buzz he was getting and wanted to find deeper experiences. He regularly went online and discovered a lot of spiritual stuff on the Web that he could experiment with. There wasn't one particular religion or philosophy that he was interested in; he took bits from each of them when he felt something would lead to a spiritual experience. He had no accountability to anyone. If it felt good, that was enough for him to embrace it.

A couple of weeks after his interest in self-improvement had begun, Cheraser was spending more and more time finding information or practising techniques. His life was absorbed in it. He was getting deeper into spirituality and trying to achieve altered states of consciousness. He had researched many different spiritual ideas and now had a deep interest in self-hypnosis, spells, and anything that offered him a sense of power within himself or over others. When he meditated, he seemed to get closer to a better feeling or some mystical knowledge, and he reflected on how he could move on to the next stage.

> The fog had cleared, and even though Cheraser still couldn't see very far, he found that the pathway was amazingly wide and very easy to walk upon. He had struggled to make any real progress along it before, but now it seemed different.
>
> 'I know we have moved you off the pathway quickly before and told you it was a waste of time, but we had to

make sure you were serious,' said Lutocc. 'There are actually two pathways. You have been on the wide path since you were conceived, but you had reached a part of your journey where you could have considered moving to a narrow one. This would have been uncomfortable for you. You are still on the right path and completely safe.'

A roar of agreement arose from a mass of people that had instantly appeared. How many there were was impossible to count. Cheraser could now see further into the distance. It was like looking into a crowd from the stage of a massive open-air concert. Cheraser was startled by this, and it brought an immediate reply from Lutocc.

'Don't worry. We have always been here. You just haven't been aware of all of us. We have been given orders to help you, but you need to keep training hard. I'll show you a little more of the pathway now,' he said, enticingly.

As Cheraser looked up, a part of the crowd disappeared, and there was now an organised group of people standing in front of him. There were still too many to count. They went back along both sides of the pathway, far into the distance. The men had muscular physiques. The women were slender and sensuous. Both sexes had a beauty that was staggering. They each stood next to a cross, presumably the one which they were responsible for, and each of them held a key that could unlock the chain wrapped around the door of their cross, making access through it possible. These doorways opened to different forms of pleasure and fulfilment.

Cheraser recognised a couple of the faces. The beautiful Stul rolled her key in an enticing way between her thumb and forefinger as she pushed strands of long black hair behind her ears. Lutocc had an aura of power as he stood by his own cross and held his key with a strong outstretched arm. A vaguely familiar keyholder unlocked the chain to his cross and opened a door to a long pathway of flashing lights and noise. He promised a good prize at the end of the journey – in return for a small entrance fee.

Another man then introduced himself.

'My name is Dreeg,' he said in an arrogant tone. His key was covered in jewels, and he quickly used it to open the door of his cross, revealing piles of money and extravagant gifts. 'My cross is just one of many which lead to happiness. Make sure that you accumulate as much money and possessions as you can.'

As Cheraser continued to walk through this stunningly good-looking crowd of people, he felt compelled to look at some keyholders while not being interested in others. Some of the promises and excitement offered were attractive, others he wasn't interested in, and some just seemed to be bad. He also noticed that there were keyholders who were responsible for things such as sport, television, cinema, and music. Cheraser found this very confusing. The promise of happiness seemed to come from good things, bad things, and things that seemed to be neither good nor bad. As he tried to communicate his confusion, a new group of hundreds spoke reassuringly in one voice to ease his fears.

'All of these things are good, but people have different preferences,' they said, slowly and clearly in a kind tone. 'Even the things you think are bad are good. Your opinions will change on these things as you progress on your journey,' they added convincingly.

They then bellowed out praise to the keyholders, who smiled in proud appreciation. Cheraser now had a strong desire to experience some of this hedonism, and he noticed that a couple of keyholders who had given him a bad vibe at first no longer affected his inner being with a sense of badness.

Lutocc then took hold of Cheraser's hand and showed him a cluster of smaller keys, under his main key, which unlocked the chains to crosses that went deeper and further away from his main one. The crosses that had originally been surrounded with a sense of darkness and fear now seemed lighter and almost peaceful. Lutocc helped Cheraser through the doorway of his main cross, unlocked another chain, and lifted Cheraser effortlessly through a second doorway. This was obviously the next level of awareness. A sense of intrigue and excitement about what he might discover compelled him to embrace the journey, and he made a conscious decision to travel with Lutocc as his guide.

Cheraser's finger hovered momentarily over the computer mouse. He had started by looking into self-improvement ideas, but this was different. He hadn't been aware of the progression. This was no longer a fleeting look at spirituality but a deep and enticing journey. The adrenaline started to pump, and he could feel his heart pounding as the anticipation grew.

He quickly clicked the 'OK to Enter' button, and there before him was a mass of information on the occult: witchcraft, Ouija boards, and astral projection along with a host of other philosophies, alternative therapies, and religions. All of them seemed to offer something that might fill the spiritual vacuum that Cheraser felt within himself. Maybe this was what he had been searching for.

2.

Challenged by Integrity

Cheraser still enjoyed his normal interests, such as going to the pub, listening to music, and playing and watching sport. If the England football team played in a big tournament, the unity he felt with the whole country was still all that mattered – until they inevitably threw it away again around the quarter finals, usually losing on penalties or something else put down to misfortune. This always left Cheraser with an empty feeling, as if it really was important. The illusion of strangers who felt like friends was ruined again, just like the feeling on New Year's Day after a night out on New Year's Eve.

He would now rather be alone for longer periods and spend hours on the Internet looking into a religion or occult practice. The intimacy and peace that he craved had actually led to more isolation from others. His mind was in turmoil, revolving around his own search for peace and enjoyment. This search was based on short-term good experiences, both in hobbies and his spiritual life, but Cheraser still felt a deep-seated sense of dissatisfaction. However, he did feel that he was closer to finding out the truth about the reason for existence – or, rather, what that truth was for him. He thought he could find it through the journey of self-discovery, and he felt the need to look even deeper into himself. He needed to find self-worth by his achievements and fill the spiritual vacuum in his life with any kind of spiritual power that gave him back control over his own destiny, whether that was through religion, philosophy, a relationship, or just sex.

After a morning surfing the Net, Cheraser glanced at the clock and couldn't believe the hours had passed by so quickly. He hadn't eaten, and he would soon have to leave the house for what was normally the highlight of his week. He played football for a club in a local league on a Saturday afternoon, and a teammate would be picking him up shortly. The games consisted of a lot of swearing, and the team ethos was to try and wind up the opposition and come off the pitch with a win at any cost. A victory gave a sense of power and importance, and an excuse for a celebration drink later in the evening, although losing also provided a good reason for a drink.

Cheraser turned off his computer reluctantly. His desire to keep reading online shocked him, in a way, as he loved football, but he felt that he was just about to uncover some spiritual truth. This knowledge seemed to be tantalizingly just out of reach, and he felt frustrated as he threw his kit into his bag. The sound of a car horn and music blaring outside signalled the arrival of his lift, and he squeezed into the back of an already nearly full vehicle, with his bag squashed between his slightly open legs.

Today was going to be a strange game. Cheraser's team thrived on arguing with the referee and the opposition, but the team that they were playing today were not like that. They had been in the same league for a couple of seasons and had built up something of a reputation for being a bit different. There was rarely any swearing from this team, and they didn't get involved with much of the nasty banter that happened in most other games – although in the nature of the sport, tempers occasionally boiled over. Apparently they were a Christian-based team, whatever that meant, and they tried to play the game with respect to the referee and the opposition.

Some members of the other teams were indifferent to this team, and others were suspicious about who they were and what they were doing. This, after all, was about football, and many in the league seemed to think that it should have nothing to do with anyone's religious beliefs. Cheraser enjoyed playing against this team, though, and admired them, although he didn't admit this to anyone. They played hard, but tried to play in a good spirit. They were friendly but not falsely nice, and they liked a laugh and a joke, without being malicious.

The trip to the opposition's ground was only a couple of miles, and Cheraser was thankful to fall out of the cramped car on arrival.

The game was only twenty minutes old when one of Cheraser's teammates received a nasty injury; an accidental collision left a deep cut just below his knee. The normal reaction from the opposition would be to tell him to get up or moan at the referee to get him off the pitch so that the game could continue – but today it was the opposition who quickly called for the game to be stopped.

Cheraser's team, as usual, had only just scraped together enough players for the starting team and hadn't brought along any supporters who could double as a physiotherapist. But it didn't matter, as someone on the sidelines from the opposition quickly ran on with water and an assortment of bandages. It was soon clear that the wound required stitches, and with no one to take the player to the local hospital, and a long period of the game to go, an opposition supporter offered to give him a lift.

Cheraser was stunned by this kindness. Normally, if someone received an injury, they were taken off the pitch and basically forgotten about. They could take no further part in the game and so were no longer important.

As the game resumed, Cheraser looked around at his own teammates, who seemed unmoved by this sportsmanship and generosity. The swearing and dislike for the other team continued. But Cheraser had been affected; he liked the fact that his teammate had been treated with compassion as a human being and not seen as an enemy in some kind of sports war.

The ten men of Cheraser's team were well beaten, and they headed to the clubhouse for a shower and some refreshments that had been provided by the opposition. This hospitality was something rarely found at any other team in the league, and a few drinks and snacks gave a welcome energy boost.

After a game, it was customary to hang around with your own teammates and not have much to do with the opposition, but the team today seemed approachable, and Cheraser felt drawn to conversation. He thanked them for their earlier actions and talked about their common interest, football. Cheraser liked the way the opposition played the game and his own team's continual moaning and lack of unity frustrated him. He enquired half-jokingly whether he could join the opposition team and was surprised when their player-manager said he would be welcome. At this level of football, there were no contracts or fees involved, and as long as the proper procedure for signing with another club was followed, there would be no problem.

Cheraser asked about the set-up of the club and was told that they were run and managed by a group from a local church that expected high standards of behaviour and sportsmanship from the players. Cheraser asked whether he would have to go to church, which brought smiles from some of the surrounding team, who had obviously asked the same question before they had joined. Attending church was not a condition to join the team. Cheraser took the manager's number and said he would think about it.

Everyone was now starting to leave, and as Cheraser picked up his kit bag, he realised that the guy who had given him a lift had already gone. Everyone else seemed to have a full car, so Cheraser embarrassingly slipped away to catch the bus home. He wasn't particularly close to any of his teammates off the field, although when he was playing he felt he belonged, as they shared a common purpose. But this purpose wasn't enough for him. He also needed to feel a sense of unity and belonging off the pitch, as a human being, not just as a footballer. His club didn't give him that. Being left behind had hurt, and he seriously considered whether to leave the team to join today's opponent.

At home, Cheraser got ready for the almost compulsory Saturday night out. He was determined to drink plenty of lager to ease the feeling of rejection. After meeting up with his friends and having a couple of swift pints, being left behind didn't seem to be as much of a problem. In fact, it gave him a story to tell and made him the centre of attention for a while. Things were not so bad after all. He felt good and hoped, this time, that his mood would not be snatched away ruthlessly by the dawning of the next day.

Cheraser awoke the next morning with a bad headache. He steadily rose from his bed to get a glass of water, trying to keep his head as still as possible. He pushed his hands hard against his eyes to keep out the daylight that seemed to be in partnership with his pounding head, both intent on punishing him for a long night out. He collapsed back into bed, his body unwilling to move.

> The pathway seemed wider than ever, and Cheraser was quickly joined by a face he did not recognise.
>
> 'My name is Slafe. I am here to help you find the truth,' he said, in what seemed to be a very genuine manner.
>
> Slafe, like all of the other friendly men and women on the pathway, had charisma and good looks. It made them all easy to trust.
>
> 'Cheraser, it would probably be better if you didn't change to that other football team, as they'll soon have you going to church. You won't be able to enjoy yourself if you do. No drinking, no porn, no sex – absolutely no fun. They will also say that there is only one way to find the truth, and

> you will have to stop your own spiritual journey.' Slafe paused for a moment and then whispered, 'Would you like to miss out on so much?'
>
> Without even waiting for an answer, Slafe helped Cheraser through the doorway of a cross, leaving an unlocked chain dangling behind them.

As Cheraser lay in bed, he still wasn't sure what to do. Yes, there were lots of reasons for not joining the new club, and they were nagging away in his mind, pleading for him not to go. Then the power of those reasons suddenly dimmed. It was a strange feeling, but Cheraser was now certain he wanted to join them. He could always leave if it did not work out.

> Immediately, as he made his decision, he was back on the path. The familiar and gorgeous face of Stul greeted him with a smile. Lutocc was also there, but he stood silently in the background without a hint of emotion on his face.
>
> 'Don't ring the football team manager yet,' said Stul. 'You need some relaxation and intimacy first.'
>
> Cheraser was captivated and headed towards the edge of the pathway. Stul had always unlocked the chain to her cross personally, but this time she gave Cheraser his own key and included some extra keys that unlocked chains to deeper and more sensuous crosses.
>
> 'These are yours, and I will never take them back from you,' she said seductively. 'As an extra gift, Lutocc wants to give you the keys to his first two crosses. As you go deeper into training, we will give you more keys to unlock deeper crosses that lead to greater knowledge and happiness,' she added gently.
>
> Cheraser felt wanted and loved. He owned these keys, and they felt like a deep part of him. He unlocked the chain around Stul's cross and entered her doorway.

Cheraser spent a couple of hours surfing the Internet. He was searching for a mixture of porn and the occult and, on some sites, found a strange mixture of both. Nothing seemed to be that shocking, and he had a continual thirst for more and more.

As he surfed, he found himself bombarded with thoughts as to why he should stay with his own football team. He knew his teammates and got on well with them on the pitch. Maybe he didn't need to be cared about after the game. He was guaranteed a place in the side every week, and he was used to the way the club was run, even if it was not ideal. But these negative thoughts were losing their power. He still had a free choice in his own head, and he still wanted to move clubs. He left his computer and decided to ring up the manager of yesterday's opponents.

As Cheraser ended the phone call, he felt that he had done the right thing. He wasn't necessarily going to play for his new team immediately, but he was prepared to work hard in training, which took place on a Wednesday evening, to try to earn a place.

He crashed out in front of the television, and it wasn't long before he drifted into a light sleep that was occasionally disturbed by a raised voice or music from advertisements which caused him to jump suddenly, as often happens when dropping off to sleep.

> Cheraser was taken by surprise on the pathway when he felt a firm slap on the back.
>
> 'Well done,' said Slafe in a forceful but friendly tone. 'Most of the time it is wise to listen to our advice, but in this case, we were just trying to see how strong you are. You have made the right decision in moving to the new team. Remember though, you don't need to change your character. Just be yourself. This can be a part of your spiritual journey. At this club, there may be a couple of things that will help you. It is not just a football club. But don't take them too seriously, and make sure you carry on with your own journey. There are many ways to find the truth, and what you have delved into so far is exciting and mysterious, isn't it?'
>
> It sounded good. As Slafe unlocked the chains around his cross, Cheraser walked through it effortlessly.

The phone rang for a few seconds before Cheraser was stirred from his daydreams. He shook his head quickly from side to side to find his bearings and eventually followed the ringtone that was coming from down the side of the settee. After pulling out the television remote control and one of his sister's hair bands, he eventually found his mobile phone.

He talked with a friend about the events of the previous evening and joked about why, when they are on their way home from a night out, a supermarket shopping trolley always seems to appear and then someone has to get in it and be pushed until they fall out. How do these trolleys get so far from the shops? Do people actually take their shopping home in them?

Cheraser declined his friend's offer of another night out that night. All he wanted to do was relax and go to bed early.

Wednesday evening soon came, and Cheraser wondered why he could never organise his football kit very well. Everything was either still in a bag, wet and dirty from the previous week, or he could only find an odd sock or shin pad. Getting ready this night was winding him up even more than normal.

> 'How about you just stay at home and relax,' whispered a new face. 'You could start with the new team next week. You're feeling a bit nervous, and they might not talk to a new person like you. You need to be feeling your best to deal with that. By the way, my name is Aref. I'm here to protect you.'
>
> Aref obviously cared, and he helped Cheraser through the door of his cross.

Cheraser gathered his kit together to make the short bus journey to the training facilities. But as he approached the artificial pitch outside the leisure centre, he began to feel quite fearful.

> Aref wasted no time in trying to help Cheraser as he joined him on the pathway.
>
> 'You can still go back home or even just watch from a distance. No one will care,' whispered Aref sympathetically.
>
> It seemed as though Aref would add to this point, but then he seemed unable to speak and quickly rushed off, as though he had remembered he needed to be somewhere else.

'Cheraser, I'm really glad you made it,' said Trenom, the player-manager of Revelation F.C.

Cheraser was impressed: first, by the fact that Trenom recognised him, but more so by the fact that he had remembered his name. They were the first to arrive, and Cheraser hoped that the rest of his new teammates would be as friendly.

The next few minutes were slightly awkward. As the other players arrived, they talked in small groups, and Cheraser felt isolated. They obviously knew each other well, and he didn't feel a part of it.

When Trenom eventually called everyone around, it brought some respite. Cheraser thought it was probably the start of the warm-up, so at least everyone would then be sharing a common purpose.

In fact, the reason for gathering everyone around was to welcome Cheraser. Trenom did this in a totally positive way, and whilst he was talking, most of the other players echoed his comments and gave handshakes and backslaps to Cheraser in a genuine way.

This was completely alien to Cheraser. When he had previously joined any new group, he had always felt that people ignored him, at least for a while. Maybe people acted that way because their security was threatened or they were just shy, but this group was different. Cheraser didn't ever show much emotion, and this was no exception, but he was moved by this welcome after only being part of this team for a few minutes. He felt affirmed as a human being and immediately felt a sense of belonging to this group.

Training was very competitive, but there was strong and fair discipline. There were a couple of instances of swearing that were quickly dealt with by the manager, and a few arguments caused by some nasty tackles. Cheraser, being the new guy, kept fairly quiet, but he took in everything that was going on around him.

At the end of training, everyone gathered around the manager and they all had a brief chat. A couple of people held up their hands and apologised for being out of order. The unity of the club was tangible. This all seemed a bit strange to Cheraser. He hardly ever apologised, unless it was to get back in favour with a girl he had upset, and swearing and bad tackles on a football pitch were part of the culture. The friendliness and feeling of belonging that he felt had challenged him though, and he wanted to be a part of this team.

As this was a church-based club, Cheraser had expected some sort of religious input, but this hadn't been the case. He was still slightly wary that they only wanted him to join so that they could preach at him; however, they seemed to be genuinely interested in him as a person, without any other agenda.

Most of the team now headed to the leisure centre bar for a drink. Cheraser joined them and was given a copy of the club rules by the manager. As Cheraser gulped down a refreshing pint, he skimmed through the written ethos of the team, the likes of which he had never seen before. Most of the rules were about having respect for your team, the opposition's team, and the match officials. Swearing during training and matches was something that the club didn't appreciate.

The rules were unusual, but this team wasn't soft. They were passionate about doing well.

Cheraser expressed his concern that he wouldn't always be able to keep these rules. Swearing, for one thing, was a normal part of his language. Trenom, the manager, then explained that everyone gets it wrong sometimes. But, as a club, they had high standards of conduct. They would discipline where necessary, but only out of care for the individual and the team.

Again, Cheraser felt affirmed by this. He felt he could be himself, and he didn't have to be a robot of false niceness that would replace his own personality. He knew he would have to watch his behaviour, but he also knew that if he made a mistake it would be dealt with in the right way.

Cheraser had assumed that most of the team members were connected to the church, but as he talked with Trenom, he was surprised to learn otherwise. The leadership team of the manager, coach, treasurer, and secretary all were, along with some of the players, but the rest were not. There was no noticeable favouritism, and everyone seemed to respect the club ethos. Saturday could not come quickly enough.

A Friday evening phone call from Trenom left Cheraser feeling disappointed. He had been named as a substitute and would not be starting the game. It was a fair decision. He understood that he was the new guy, but he had always been used to playing every week.

> The friendly voice of Lutocc on the pathway dulled the pain as he introduced a new friend.
>
> 'This is Treger. He has some advice for you,' said Lutocc.
>
> 'Cheraser, maybe you shouldn't have left your old team,' Treger whispered sympathetically. 'What if you never get in the new team?' Then he disappeared, leaving an air of confusion.
>
> 'Treger is a bit of a worrier, so just use the keys I gave you to take your mind off things,' added Lutocc in a caring tone.
>
> The advice was appealing, and as Cheraser reached for his keys, he noticed that he now had three. Lutocc had generously added another. Cheraser unlocked the chains on the doorways of three crosses, each took him deeper inside.

Cheraser's head was buzzing when he finally turned off his computer around 3.00 a.m. There were so many theories on having a mystical experience, and he craved the feeling of power. As he drifted off to sleep, his dreams were of a spiritual nature. He dreamt he was floating high above the ground, and he felt an immense feeling of freedom. It was a euphoric and highly enjoyable experience.

When he awoke just before midday, a depression greeted him with an ugly smile. He knew he would need some more keys from Lutocc to find freedom again. It was going to be an exhausting and demanding journey. He felt he was in no state to be playing football. It was almost a relief to know that he was going to be a substitute.

When the game actually started, the disappointment of not playing returned. He did however get on the pitch for the last twenty minutes and played well. He was determined to work hard to gain a place in the starting line up. The squad was fairly small, and he knew that, with injuries and unavailability, his chance would eventually come.

3.

An Alien Culture

The last seven weeks had been difficult for Cheraser. For most people, playing football in the rain on a muddy pitch with only about ten people watching you would not be that appealing. But football was almost a religion to Cheraser, and he had just started and played his first full game for Revelation F.C.

Everything in life seemed to be pretty good. He had three separate lives. He had his spiritual life where he searched in secret for something to fill his hole of emptiness within. He had his mates who he could get drunk with. And he had the football team where he felt valued. He enjoyed all of these lives, and he was a different person in each of these areas.

Cheraser was a great people watcher and had noticed that the football club ethos rubbed off on everyone involved. He was now in the habit of not swearing whilst training and playing. It was strange how he had started to take on some of the characteristics of the group.

There was certainly something different about the leaders. They were strong but not controlling. They also seemed to care about each individual, without requiring anything in return. The personality of each player was nurtured and not suppressed. For example, one of the lads, who had originally been a bit mouthy and full of himself, was now the captain of the team. He was still mouthy, but this characteristic was now being used in a positive way. He wasn't connected to the church but had taken on the club ethos, and he was the first to have a word with you if you were out of order. And the quieter ones were asked to look after the kit or to send in match reports to the local paper. Everyone at the club could get involved in some way if they wanted to, increasing again the sense of ownership and unity. Of course this wasn't some cotton wool dreamland, and there were disagreements and problems, but they always seemed to be dealt with in a fair way.

Cheraser obviously made the assumption that some of the club principles came from its connection with the church. This led him to ponder what a Christian was.

> Slafe was waiting for him on the pathway.
>
> 'Cheraser, I will open the chain of a doorway that leads through a new cross. This is the cross that leads to freedom by being good,' Slafe whispered. 'Good deeds and being nice will help you, but remember; you can take bits from all kinds of teachings to help you on your spiritual journey.'
>
> He then pushed Cheraser through the door of the cross.

Cheraser made sense of it in his own head. A Christian, he presumed, was someone who did good things. He thought he had done pretty well: he hadn't killed anyone or stolen anything in his life. He was happy to play the good guy around the football team, and he enjoyed the company of most of the squad, although, there are always some people you don't particularly like or connect with.

This club was not just a football team. They organised many social activities. They could often be found at Indian or Chinese restaurants, the cinema, or a bowling alley. It was a sociable group to be involved with.

His teammates were the only connection Cheraser had with Christianity, and although he was still slightly wary of them, they seemed to be very genuine people who loved life and invested time in relationships with others. He knew other people and groups who had nothing to do with Christianity who were just as caring, but he now knew some Christians and had a positive view about them.

As Cheraser sat down in the changing room for the customary after-game chat from the manager, the mist from the hot showers and the pungent aroma of various deodorants could almost be digested. After some encouraging words following their 2 – 0 victory, Trenom had a couple of notices. The first was about the next social gathering at a pizza restaurant and then there were details about some kind of church event. Apparently, there was a special service coming up, a week from tomorrow, and the players were invited. It was to be held at a local community centre, not the church, and started at 10.00 a.m. A few flyers were then passed around to advertise the event.

Cheraser was surprised at the response from the other players or, rather, the lack of response from them. There were no jokes or banter about it, just a complete silence for a few seconds. Then everyone gathered their kit and headed to the bar for a drink, leaving most of the flyers behind.

Cheraser was side by side with Slafe on the pathway.

> 'I told you they only wanted you to join the team so that they could get you into church. Maybe you should go; it may help with your spiritual journey. But remember, a 10.00 a.m. start on a Sunday, following a late night on a Saturday, is not a great idea,' said Slafe quietly, with a reassuring arm around Cheraser. Slafe unlocked the chain to his cross and helped Cheraser through the door.

The sounds of glasses being set gently onto the table and the crunching noise of a packet of crisps landing on his lap brought Cheraser out of his thoughts and back to the reality of his surroundings. There was an embarrassing non-discussion about the church service from the other players. There seemed to be little interest from anyone.

Cheraser wondered if all the friendliness at the club was some kind of love bombing, leading up to this invite to the community centre. But he was thinking more and more about spirituality, and he sort of wanted to go, just out of curiosity. Maybe it would help in his search for a spiritual experience. The Christian guys here were normal everyday people who didn't force their opinions of spiritual truth onto others. There was never a short religious talk woven uncomfortably, in a clashing colour, around the team's football kit. The principles of their faith were spoken about boldly, but always in natural circumstances.

Cheraser glanced furtively at the flyer he had been given. It had a wet glass mark on it and was covered in fragments of crisps. It appeared that the aim of the service was to give people an opportunity to learn more about Christianity. The flyer gave Cheraser a clear idea of what he would be letting himself in for if he went along, and he didn't feel under any pressure to attend. It was much better than having a spiritual message thrust at him unexpectedly when all he had come along to do was play football. Perhaps the friendship of the football club leadership was really genuine. It seemed that his attendance or non-attendance at the service wouldn't affect his place in the team.

Cheraser weighed it all up in his mind and then expressed an interest in attending to Trenom, who offered to give him a lift to the community centre. Cheraser had never been to a church service before, apart from his mum's third wedding, and he was rather looking forward to it. But he did want to be seated somewhere near the back so that he could make a quick exit if he needed to.

During the next week, he was sometimes certain that he wanted to go to the service and then, a short time later, he was just as certain that he didn't want to go. He finally decided that he would make a decision on the day of the event. His mood and feelings could fight each other until then, and depending on the winner of the civil war within, he would either stay in bed or get up at a time on a Sunday morning that he hadn't seen since he was at primary school.

On Saturday, Cheraser enjoyed another drink-fuelled escape from reality, but at the back of his mind, he knew he needed to be up early the next morning, as Trenom was picking him up for the church service. It seemed strange that he was here in a nightclub, with people drinking and dancing, and yet in a few hours would be in a community centre, sort of at church. He almost felt a touch of guilt at the thought of it, but he was good at changing who he was, depending on his surroundings. At this moment, though, he wished that Trenom was not coming to pick him up for the service. It would then be easier not to go. The thought of an early rise was spoiling his night, and to the surprise of his mates, he made an early exit for home and bed.

When the alarm went off on Sunday morning, Cheraser's eyelids felt like they were cemented somewhere near the bottom of his face, and going to something that resembled church did not seem appealing at all. His warm duvet was a companion he really didn't want to be separated from.

> The pathway was strangely quiet and deserted. Cheraser quickly left through the unlocked doorway of a cross, with no keyholder in sight.

There was no way he could really get out of it now. Cheraser didn't like to let people down, and he was being picked up in twenty minutes.

He missed breakfast, and when Trenom arrived slightly early, Cheraser, hoping he didn't look too much of a mess, joined him in the car.

The journey to the community centre was awkward. Cheraser wasn't sure if any of the other football lads were going, and he was a little uneasy about what the morning ahead had in store for him. Trenom was usually chatty, and although he was still friendly today, he seemed to be struggling to think of things to say. It was a relief when they arrived at the centre.

They were greeted in the car park by a lot of people who were all wearing fluorescent jackets with the word ‘Steward’ printed on the back. All of them seemed to be carrying walkie-talkie radios and were walking around the car park hurriedly, for no apparent reason. This wasn’t some kind of sell-out concert for a famous band; it was a small church service. The car park was big, so there was no need for any help in finding a space. This army of the self-important actually made parking more difficult, as they blinded all the drivers with their glaring outer garment. Their attire was either just overbearing officiousness or the church’s attempt to follow its mission statement by arranging a modernist fashion show. There was a lot of arm waving and confusion, and Trenom eventually found a spot that was acceptable to the almost robotic stewards. The whole thing was way over the top. Cheraser found it extremely funny. It seemed to be so unnecessary and false.

> Cheraser was helped into a comfortable, almost throne-like, chair by a group of small, hyperactive people who didn’t say a word. They just giggled. As they dispersed into the distance, the friendly face of Slafe appeared, and he pulled Cheraser from the comfort of the chair.
>
> ‘Come and see this group of new crosses that I have for you. The chains are already unlocked, and they lead the way to some important knowledge,’ said Slafe.
>
> Cheraser looked closely at one of the crosses. It seemed to be very lightweight and made from cheap material. He was reluctant to walk through it, as he only wanted to enter a doorway to an authentic wooden cross. Sensing his reluctance to proceed, Slafe had a word of encouragement for him.
>
> ‘You will not be hurt if you embrace this group of crosses. They will cause confusion as you walk through each doorway, but this will be a good thing. It will help you in your search for truth.’
>
> Cheraser hesitantly walked through the doorway of the nearest cross.

Cheraser stared quizzically at the community centre, as Trenom locked his car and double checked the door handle two or three times to make sure it was secure.

Why was the service being held here? All other weeks, it was at the church – but not this week. Did they have something to hide, or were new people not good enough to enter the normal church building?

There may have been a good reason for having the service at this place, but nothing had been communicated. Cheraser wondered if the people here were just not being themselves. Maybe they were trying to hype something up and sell him a product that he didn't feel he wanted to own.

He was a little guarded as he approached the front door, and before he could open it himself, it was swung open by an over-friendly steward. The steward's smile seemed to extend his face to twice its natural size, and his handshake was unnervingly accompanied by a bear hug. Cheraser, who had barely managed to stay on his feet, was then overwhelmed by a number of people simultaneously saying hello and handing him an assortment of books and sheets of paper that he struggled to keep hold of. As he fought through this shield of human chaos, and feeling as though he had just left a library, he was disappointed to see that the back row of seats had already been filled, mostly by old people. He sat just in front of them with Trenom and was relieved to be sitting in the relative safety of an uncomfortable plastic chair.

The community centre filled up, and eventually some activity at the front ended a period of strange background music. There was some shuffling around as problems with a microphone were sorted out, but then came a welcome, loud and clear, presumably from the vicar. As the church minister continued, he instructed everyone to introduce themselves to someone nearby who they didn't know.

The intention was obviously to break the ice, but it had the opposite effect on Cheraser. He was rubbish at small talk, and he moved around nervously in his seat, trying not to make eye contact with another person. He didn't talk to anyone, apart from Trenom, who seemed to be just as uncomfortable.

Some musicians then got onto the stage. They were a mix of old and young people and looked to be a family affair, as the majority looked amazingly similar to each other. The music was not what Cheraser expected. There were no hymns; the sound was not really old-fashioned, but neither was it current. It was almost a culture of its own, with certain hand actions and dancing at times, like some kind of annoying novelty record. Some people seemed to be aware of these actions but not everyone. It all felt rather exclusive.

Cheraser felt like he was an outsider being told to do things he didn't feel comfortable with. He didn't want to become a clone of church. He knew the songs mentioned God and Jesus, but he had no real understanding of what they were about. The person standing to the left of Cheraser raised her arms in the air, invading his personal space, and at times nearly hit him in the face. This was not only distracting but just weird. He also felt embarrassed as he shuffled through all the books and papers he had been given, trying to find the words to each song before they were halfway through. He mouthed the words as he watched the other people gathered there.

It was amazing how many patterned jumpers and cardigans were being worn by young and old alike, and there were a few brightly coloured T-shirts that advertised Christian festivals or events, with the year of the event giving away the age of the clothing. There were also quite a few women wearing floral dresses with ankle socks. Cheraser enjoyed fairly fashionable clothes and couldn't see himself being a part of this group. He presumed he would have to turn into one of these clones if he attended regularly, which he didn't want to do anyway. Again, it was reinforced in his own mind that this was a culture all of its own – and not a very appealing one.

The singing eventually came to an end and was followed by a completely unfunny drama sketch in which the so-called actors shouted a lot in high-pitched voices. The whole thing was so bad that Cheraser could only stare down at his own feet in embarrassment. Whatever message he was supposed to get escaped him because he had switched off long before the end. This was what the word *cringe* had been invented for, and every time Cheraser looked at his watch he was sure it had gone backwards.

A short video clip accompanied by a well-known song brought some light relief, but this was spoilt by a few of the older people in the back row who talked throughout, complaining that the music was too loud and that they couldn't see the screen. They had chatted all through the service as well about not being able to hear! Cheraser wondered why they hadn't sat at the front. After all, they had probably been up since 6.00 a.m. and been first to arrive at the community centre, so they'd had plenty of time to choose their seats.

The vicar then rejoined the stage. It was obviously time for him to talk, hopefully, not for too long. The whole message was about giving away some of your money. Cheraser cynically thought that the church must be short of some, and this was a fund-raising exercise. He switched off and relived yesterday's football match in his mind instead.

He was awoken from his thoughts when the vicar urged anyone who wanted to become a Christian to either read the booklet that was amongst the pile of papers everyone had been given on entry or to talk to him or one of the other leaders, who had nice big name badges to identify them.

The service ended, and before Cheraser had time to read the booklet, some stewards barged along each row to collect song sheets and other stuff that needed to be put away quickly, presumably so that a few roast dinners did not overcook. They were obviously trying to be helpful, but this had disrupted any thinking time that may have been required. Cheraser did just manage to keep hold of the booklet, even though he planned to throw it away. He really wasn't interested. He was open to spiritual things, but he hadn't connected with this at all. He preferred a more interactive approach to learning, where he was involved and could ask questions. Of course, he went to the cinema or occasionally to the theatre, which were similar set-ups to this service, but those were for entertainment. This service was about learning in his opinion, not entertainment, and there had been too much time spent preaching at him and telling him what to believe. He wanted to know what their opinion was, but he also needed to feel included, to be a part of what was going on, and to have some input and thinking time. This whole thing had been too long, irrelevant, and not authentic.

As Trenom and Cheraser left the building, they were subjected to another wall of smiles and handshakes. The only thing missing was a few babies having their heads kissed and then it would have looked just like a political party canvassing for votes. Cheraser had seen this kind of behaviour in sales people and politicians, and he didn't trust it for a minute. He was handed a leaflet as he left, advertising a course on Christianity, but he wanted none of it. The whole thing was uninspiring and dry.

The journey back with Trenom was quiet, and Cheraser was relieved to get home and do what he normally did on a Sunday – lay in bed.

> Slafe welcomed Cheraser as he wearily walked upon the pathway.

'Relax, Cheraser. I will protect you now. Just remember not to get involved with any more of these church activities. Just stick to the football. The church is boring and false. What I said before is obviously wrong. They will not help you with your spiritual journey. I will help you find the truth,' Slafe whispered. Then he unlocked a chain to one of his crosses.

Cheraser entered and fell into a deep and dreamless sleep.

4.

Cloned Vision

Revelation Football Club had been in existence for four years. It was a team that had been set up by a man who attended a local church, and the team carried the church's name. The man's name was Trenom, and his vision was to provide a Christian testimony in the world of local football. He therefore wanted to make sure that Christian principles were of the utmost importance to the ethos of the club. You didn't have to claim to be a Christian to be eligible to play for Revelation FC, but you did need to adhere to the principles that were central to what the club was about. The manager and most of the club committee were Christians, as were some of the players, and this ensured the continuation of the ethos.

Trenom had originally wanted to get a group of people together who had a common passion so that good relationships could be developed between them. He felt that it was important to breed a feeling of unity, belonging, and purpose in an environment where people could be honest with each other and discover the truth about Christianity in a natural way. He had a faith that had changed his life, and he wanted people to discover that for themselves.

Trenom had the backing of his church to set up the club, which gave him some accountability for the way the team was managed, but from the very beginning, he had a major concern that he knew would cause problems in the future. His concern was that many people at the church thought that the football club would be a great way of recruiting more people into the Sunday morning church service.

Trenom knew that as a Christian he needed to meet together with other believers in some form. He was passionate about his relationship with God, but he found church services difficult to engage with and often irrelevant, even though he had attended from a young age and been immersed in church culture for so long. He wanted to share his faith with the football team and see each player understand and accept what he believed to be the truth about God, but he knew that if anyone did, they would probably struggle to embrace church life. Some of the leadership team at Revelation Church saw regular attendance at the main Sunday service as essential to real faith, and so, with Trenom at odds with this concept, clashes were inevitable.

If growth was to happen in the church, Trenom believed something needed to change. God's saving plan for mankind never changed, but maybe the way Christians communicated the truth of that plan to spiritual searchers did need to, not just to follow the latest evangelical trend or fashion for the sake of it or to dilute the truth in any way, but to enable the gospel message to be accessible to those who found church culture a barrier to faith. Trenom guessed that there were probably many people wanting to explore Christianity, but because they felt alienated by church and church activities, they searched for spiritual meaning elsewhere.

Trenom had seen many young people struggle to engage with church over a long period of time. He knew that sitting uncomfortably for an hour and a half in a church service, without much interaction, was mostly a waste of time for them. The highlight of their morning was sending messages on their mobile phones or talking amongst themselves. They weren't being intentionally rebellious, but perhaps they would never grow into relating to this traditional model of worship. At this church, the young people had a separate youth meeting, but when they became too old to attend the youth meetings, they tended to drift away from church life altogether and give up on their faith.

A Revelation Church service consisted of singing, preaching, readings, and the occasional drama. Everyone sat in rows of uncomfortable chairs, which had replaced the original rows of uncomfortable pews. There had been much discussion and argument over the years about the content of Sunday morning services, the style of music, in particular, and there was now a strange mix of the old and the contemporary. This was a valid form of worship, but despite the changes, it was still only relevant to a small number of people who were generally older and had attended church for a long time and who worshipped and learnt in a more traditional way.

Trenom thought that the debate over the content of church services pinpointed a much more serious issue than just personal preference. His opinion was that his church had become a sub-culture all of its own, so far removed from most of popular culture that it even disengaged some of its own members. What chance, then, was there to engage any possible newcomers?

The problem was that, when Trenom originally started the football club, he knew he wanted to share his Christian faith, but he had no idea how to integrate new Christians into the church. Maybe he should have expressed his concerns to the minister and other leaders right at the beginning, but he unwisely avoided the issue, fearing that they would suggest an open-air service on the football pitch with a selection of hymns and poetry readings. It was now four years later, and some problems were beginning to surface.

There had been some rumblings for a while from some of the church members about the football team. It always seemed to be polite talk, but the conversation carried an invisible serrated edge that undermined and alienated Trenom, cutting down his enthusiasm. The questions were all of a similar theme. Why were none of the footballers ever seen in church? How many had become Christians? Was this form of friendship evangelism becoming too separate from the church?

In some ways, Trenom hated the term *friendship evangelism*. It seemed to mean that you were only being friendly with people so that you could try and convert them, and if after a while there was no conversion, it would be time to move on to another unsuspecting target. Where was the real friendship and love in that?

Trenom wanted authentic friendships, not conditional relationships dependant on others accepting the gospel message as truth. Of course, he wanted to share his faith, but then it was a free will choice for people to accept or reject what he was claiming to be the truth.

None of the football lads had become Christians, but Trenom knew it was not like the former days of evangelism. In those times, a Bible holding preacher would have bellowed out the Christian message to a crowd. The children and young people in attendance would have been dressed identically to their parents and grandparents, and there would have been conversions from the whole spectrum of ages. On some occasions, instant conversion probably still did happen. But now, in a much-changed world with a cynical and untrusting generation, the pathway to faith was a much longer journey.

As for the players never being seen in church, this left Trenom with a certain amount of guilt. He had shielded them away from the services as much as possible, as he didn't see the bridging of football club to church service as essential. His heart wanted them to come into a relationship with God and for them to meet with other believers in some form, but he still didn't know the answer to how this could be done effectively. The church had run a few courses on the basics of Christianity, with the aim of helping people find faith and fellowship with other believers, but this fellowship ultimately meant the weekly service.

A few of the football lads had been on one of these courses, but they just hadn't been able to relate. There was some time for interaction and discussion, but the content was still quite preachy and packaged for a quick conversion. Trenom knew that this type of course was relevant to a certain kind of person, one who was ready to hear some answers in a structured format. But, for many, this spiritual first-aid box wouldn't provide the relevant metaphorical long-term treatment.

Trenom also knew that spiritual searchers needed the support of Christians who were willing to travel with them over the long term and who would listen to the stories of those seeking truth and give them space to ask questions in their own time. It wasn't helpful to force anyone onto the church conveyor belt to instant conversion.

Trenom voiced his concerns to the church leadership, but he didn't feel as though they understood him. Because he cared passionately about the people involved in the football club, he did not push the church's agenda, and the team and the church became increasingly separated.

The church leadership had now become concerned about a missing generation in the church. There were very few people representing the age group which stretched from late teenagers to early thirties, and a service was being planned that would hopefully be of interest to this particular group. There was a polite pressure on church members to bring along someone they knew, and as Trenom was in contact with many people from this age range, he was singled out for a meeting with the leadership. As so often happened in this kind of meeting, all the words spoken were supposedly said in love, but Trenom knew that the leadership would be watching to see how many players from the football team attended the planned service. Some flyers were going to be printed to advertise this fast-moving presentation, and Trenom was politely told that he needed to make sure that every person connected with Revelation Football Club received a personal invite.

Trenom dreaded this kind of service, as it seemed that everyone was watching out for those who had brought along the most victims. When these events were organised properly, they could sometimes be good. Music, film clips and other multi-media methods were great ways to communicate the Christian message, but they were often mixed in with old-fashioned church culture and had an edge that seemed quite false. There was always a change of venue for these events which seemed to suggest that non-Christians weren't allowed into the proper church building. The outcome was normally just the same old church service, but in a community centre.

After meeting with the church leadership, Trenom travelled straight to the home ground of Revelation FC. Today was match day, and he was late arriving. He hadn't wanted a meeting right before a game, as he knew it would probably drag on for far too long. He had been right and was now in a bad mood.

His displeasure was heightened by the fact that he didn't enjoy playing against today's opponents. They had a nasty side to their game and an arrogance that often left some bad feelings at the end of the match. Trenom didn't feel like showing much good spirit, and a bit of an argument with the opposition seemed a tempting prospect. Of course, this wasn't a good example of the club ethos, but as the game started, Trenom knew that the slightest provocation could create an opportunity for him to vent his bubbling inner anger in an uncharacteristic show of outward aggression.

The game was fairly uneventful, though, until one of the opposition received a nasty injury in an accidental collision. The game carried on, but Trenom suddenly snapped out of his dark mood and remembered what this club was all about. He shouted to the referee to stop the game. After the injury was assessed, it was obvious that the player needed stitches. There was no one connected with the opposition watching the game, so Trenom arranged for one of his mates from the church, who had been on the sidelines, to take the player to the local accident and emergency department.

As play carried on, it didn't seem like anyone from the opposition really cared about their injured player or had even noticed the kindness of the Revelation FC team, but that was a pretty normal occurrence. At least it had brought an end to Trenom's mood, and the game ended with a comfortable victory for his side.

In the clubhouse, after the game, Trenom and a few of the team struck up a conversation with one of the opposition. His name was

Cheraser; he thanked them for the way in which they had handled the injury to his teammate. He also expressed an interest in joining Revelation FC. Trenom wasn't in the habit of chasing after players from other teams, but Cheraser was free to join them if he wanted to, so he gave him his phone number.

Trenom had doubted the effectiveness of the work he had been doing with the football team, and the pressure from the church had been adding to that, so he was determined to explain the details of this incident at the church service the next day. He prepared some things to say, and there were quite a few polite smiles from the congregation as he delivered his words. It was an encouraging time, but Trenom knew that his reasons for talking did carry a certain amount of pride. He felt that he needed to prove that there was some sort of spiritual progress in the work with the football team, and maybe this would somehow quantify it. It was almost like reaching a sales target, and he felt a little uneasy.

There were some nice comments to Trenom after the service, but there were some unhelpful ones as well. One of the leaders of the church reminded him of the seeker service that was approaching and mentioned how good it would be to get Cheraser to come along. The poor lad hadn't even joined the team yet!

Later on that day, Trenom received a phone call from Cheraser. He wanted to give the team a try, and they discussed the time and venue for training. After the conversation ended, Trenom prayed that he and the other players would welcome Cheraser in a genuine way.

When Wednesday arrived, Trenom was slightly nervous as he set out the equipment for training on the artificial pitch. He was hoping Cheraser would come along and was delighted when he was first to arrive. The other players soon trickled in and talked amongst themselves, leaving Cheraser looking a little isolated. Trenom was aware that he probably felt a bit uncomfortable, so he quickly finished off his preparations and gathered everyone around to officially welcome Cheraser in front of the team. The majority of the other lads acknowledged him with a shake of the hand. Some of the others, perhaps because of shyness or insecurity, were a bit aloof. But the general mood seemed welcoming, which pleased Trenom.

Training was competitive, with a few arguments. The team leadership always tried to discuss and sort out any problems at the end of the session, and this occasion was no exception. This was a game played with passion in an imperfect and often messy world, and one of the aims of Revelation FC was to breed an attitude of forgiveness and change, rather than one of judgement and preaching.

Trenom and Cheraser discussed the club's ethos and rules after training. Trenom hoped he had effectively communicated that they were not looking for faultless robots. He wanted to affirm Cheraser's own personality and talents, but within a framework that didn't compromise what the club was about.

5.

Broken then Renewed

Seven weeks had passed since Cheraser had joined the team. He had fit in with the group very quickly. Trenom liked his cheeky, fun-loving nature and the fact that he respected the principles of the club. He had trained well, so Trenom had him in the starting line up today after seeing him put in a few decent performances as a substitute.

Revelation FC had just completed a 2 – 0 victory. As the players sat in the changing room, Trenom congratulated them and then reached into his bag for a tidy stack of paper held together neatly with an elastic band. A couple of days earlier, he had been given the dreaded flyers by the church secretary. They advertised the service that was to take place shortly, and he was asked to hand them out to the football lads. There was always a polite indifference and quietness amongst the team whenever any church activity was mentioned. Very rarely was anyone interested.

Trenom first talked about the next social event, a trip to the local pizza parlour, and then handed out the flyers. He soon realised that he should have just put them straight onto thc changing room floor, as that was where most of them were left as the players headed for a drink. He picked up the soggy collage with a sigh of resignation and wondered if he should have been a bit more enthusiastic about handing them out. But he didn't really want to go himself, so creating a false enthusiasm would have shown a lack of integrity.

Trenom joined the rest of the squad for a drink. There was no mention of the service until Cheraser pulled him to one side and enquired, almost apologetically, about attending. Trenom was shocked that someone actually wanted to go but composed himself enough to offer Cheraser a lift, although he had mixed views about taking him to the service. He knew that he would be popular amongst the other church members for bringing Cheraser along, and there was a small possibility that he would find it relevant. But these services were usually awful. Was it the best thing for Cheraser? Would attending put him off ever wanting to know God? Would the good relationship that was only just beginning be spoilt by the church's well-meaning but often irrelevant attempt to give the gospel message in one hour?

Often at these types of services, it was as though the church was saying, 'I've told them about you, God. I've not listened to them or journeyed with them, but I don't feel so guilty now that I've told them.'

Maybe someone, somewhere, would find faith in God at a service like this, but was the motivation for organising it rooted in a genuine desire for them to know the truth or was it actually partly self-centred? Trenom knew that, nowadays, the journey of faith was often long and required Christians to listen to other people, not to just give them answers before they had even asked the questions.

As Trenom arrived to collect Cheraser, he did so with a certain amount of nervousness. This was outside the normal context of their relationship, and it seemed a bit awkward in the car as they travelled to the community centre. Normally, there was plenty of chat between them. But the atmosphere today was strained, and Trenom noticed that Cheraser looked as if he was suffering from the effects of a very recent night out. It was a relief when he eventually drove into the community centre car park.

That relief, however, was quickly snatched away as they were greeted by a police force of church members who were pointing out where to park in quite an aggressive manner. Dressed in their brand-new fluorescent jackets and communicating with walkie-talkie radios, when really they could have just shouted at each other, the car park stewards were incredibly officious. They may have felt good, but this did not give a good impression to visitors. A security firm should have been hired to lock them up in a prison for pretend important people.

As Trenom and Cheraser entered the community centre, they were greeted with a completely over the top welcome. They had barely made it through the door before being assaulted with a wall of teeth, handshakes, and pats on the back. Ironically, some of these door stewards were normally pretty miserable. Trenom wondered why, if they were naturally miserable, they couldn't just stay like that. It didn't seem quite right to change just for today.

After being handed a bagful of paperwork, Trenom and Cheraser made it safely to some chairs. They were seated one row from the back, just in front of a row of elderly people. There were some great and cheerful elderly church members who Trenom adored, but there were also some who just moaned all the time. Today was no different, and they were complaining loudly enough to be heard about the change of venue and that they probably wouldn't be able to see or hear.

As he sat in awkward silence, Trenom noticed that there was a problem with the microphones. He chuckled to himself, as there seemed to be enough equipment to hold a concert at a massive stadium. There was a lot of activity at the front from flustered church members, who obviously had put a lot of effort into making this happen; but was it necessary? The church building had a sound and visual system built in. If the event had been held there, maybe it would have been more relaxed and the people more focused, without all the frantic busyness. The problems were fortunately sorted out quickly, and after the minister had welcomed everyone, he went straight into the icebreaker.

Everyone should have then put on their thermals and ski hats because this should have been renamed the *icemaker*. The idea was to say hello to people you didn't know. Trenom felt real sympathy for Cheraser, and he was embarrassed by this cringe-inducing start. If you went to a new friend's house, would they immediately make you say hello to all of their neighbours?

The worship group then got up to lead everyone in song. This was fine for those who enjoyed music, but it slightly excluded those it was aiming to reach. The songs were mostly about a personal and intimate relationship with God that already existed and were not about provoking thought. This was great for believers but not for searchers.

The service then had a near-death experience caused by a drama sketch with some terrible acting. The whole thing seemed to be a chance for a few people to show off on stage, using ridiculous high-pitched voices and laughing amongst themselves. This was followed by some images accompanied by a well-known pop song, which provoked some thought, but was slightly spoilt by some mumblings from the older generation who obviously didn't find it relevant.

The event finally had a cardiac arrest as the minister gave his sermon. There was nothing wrong with it in the context of people who were already in a relationship with God, but the theme was tithing. Giving away ten percent of what you receive was totally irrelevant for a searcher service. But the church had themes planned out months in advance, and they weren't going to change the schedule to upset the balance of their own programme. No one had thought this through when the searcher service was being planned. Any newcomers must have got the impression that God and church just wanted to get your money.

As the service ended, the minister finished off by saying that, if anyone wanted to become a Christian, they should read the booklet they had been given or should talk to someone with a name badge on. He had barely finished talking before a group of well meaning stewards swarmed around like agitated wasps to collect song sheets and the like. There had been no time for any sort of reflection, and the offer of a cup of tea or coffee from another irritating steward meant that any spiritual searcher immediately switched off from all thoughts of a spiritual nature.

Trenom just wanted to get Cheraser out of the place, and they tried to make a quick exit by battling through another wall of grins and handshakes. In the process of getting through this human perimeter fence of irritating, glued-on smiles, they were handed a leaflet advertising an introductory course about Christianity. Trenom noticed that it was like being given a flyer in a town centre. There was no real eye contact or personal interest at all; just a frantic need to make sure everyone passing by received one. It kind of summed up the whole thing, a duty rather than something genuine. Maybe people did truly desire that others found faith in God, but this had seemed dry and legalistic, more like a holiday sales seminar than an authentic interest in other people.

The service had been a confusing mix of church culture and popular culture, falseness and realness, egos and serving, and a desire to give searchers all the answers before they had even asked the questions relevant to them. It was like a production line ending in a pre-packaged course with the main purpose of turning people into spiritual robots. If people didn't attend this course, then at least some of the church members felt that they had done their duty. Trenom knew that most spiritual seekers wouldn't come to any follow-on event. This probably wasn't because of their complete rejection or disinterest in spiritual matters: it was because the real truth of the gospel message was far away and blurred, as if the searchers were short-sighted and had forgotten their glasses.

Trenom gave Cheraser a lift home. The short journey was an uncomfortable ride because of the tense atmosphere created by an awkward silence. Trenom tried to think of something to say that would bring some humour to the moment, but his brain seemed unable to turn a muddle of thoughts into any kind of audible speech.

As Cheraser got out of the car, Trenom felt a sense of relief that he was now gone. But he also had a conflicting feeling of hopelessness, as he wondered if he had spoilt a genuine friendship by taking Cheraser to a church service that was not right or relevant for him.

Trenom felt very emotional and had just about held back his tears until he got to his front door. As soon as he opened it, he sobbed before God. He poured out all his frustrations and his anger. He had a passion to let people know the truth about God, but he just didn't know how to do this with the pressure of conforming to church culture. It crushed his heart. He knew that he couldn't convince people of their need for God, only God could do that, but he knew something about church culture had to change.

He was determined to find out how God wanted to reach out into this community through the church, in a way that was relevant to the many diverse groups of people who lived there. As he prayed and found the heart of God, he was convinced of the things wrong in his own life. He knew he had many issues. He had a bad attitude towards his church leaders and many other personal battles with wrong ways of living. He knew he was a messy kind of Christian, but he also knew that that was exactly the kind of person God used. He had a passionate heart to know God more and to share the truth about Him with others.

Trenom felt that God wanted to do some work in his life, to change his bad attitudes and other unhelpful ways of living. This wasn't about rules and regulations, being punished, or missing out. It was about freedom, truth, and sharing an intimate relationship with the creator of the world.

The next few weeks were painful as areas of Trenom's life that God needed to change were highlighted. He didn't need to work his way into acceptance and approval from his maker, and he didn't have to be perfect, just willing to let God change him and help him make the right choices.

As Trenom desperately tried to surrender his will to the purifying hand of God, he felt an even more passionate heart to love others and to show them God's love.

He eventually shared his experience with a couple of trusted, like-minded church friends, and they prayed together. They searched

God's heart for His will on how to share the truth with others in a relevant way and for wisdom on how to bring people who wanted a relationship with God into meeting with other Christians, without turning them into clones of 'churchianity'.

This wasn't just an odd few minutes of prayer with a long list of requests. It was long, regular, and intimate times of meeting with God. It meant missing out on some television programmes, a night out, and even some church meetings, but Trenom and his friends were determined to move into spiritual battle and make an impact for God.

As they spent more and more time praying, they found their motivations changing. At the beginning, they had felt in opposition to the church leaders, so they considered setting up their own way of doing things. But as the weeks went by, they realised that this wasn't the will of God. They needed to be accountable, and the leaders were God's appointed. They prayed for their leaders, and when you pray for someone, it is difficult not to love them and see them as God does. These intimate times with God broke down a lot of selfish desires, and it became clear that the church needed to seek God together for His help in reaching out into the local community.

Trenom felt it was time to share what was on his mind with the church minister who he hoped would support the idea of the whole church praying for God's heart on these issues. In Trenom's mind, he wanted some specific times arranged at church, but people could also pray individually or in small groups at home. It seemed a great idea, and Trenom and his friends had a renewed enthusiasm in their spiritual lives.

Trenom met alone with the minister, who listened attentively to the points that he raised. The minister said that he would talk to the other leaders about getting it onto the agenda of the next church members' meeting. In the meantime, Trenom and his fellow 'prayer warriors' increased their prayer time and waited for the next gathering of what could usually be described as Christian dullness.

Church meetings were normally pretty boring affairs, and this one started off in a similar way. After a few pleasant words from the minister and a token prayer, the next twenty-five minutes were taken up with a heated discussion about the colour of the church entrance. Trenom's frustration at this perceived wasting of too much time on triviality led to his unwise suggestion of pink, which didn't go down well with some of the stuffier members. Eventually, though, the next item on the agenda was about setting up a specific group to pray for the local community with an emphasis on sharing the message of Christianity in a way that was relevant to people's lives.

The first comment was about how good the last seeker service had been and how disappointing it was that no one had then started coming to church. A few other comments echoed this, and Trenom's heart sank. These people were genuine in their beliefs and in wanting to bring it to others, but they had no idea how to go about this apart from drowning others in a river of church culture.

The leaders were fairly quiet until one eventually mentioned that the weekly Thursday prayer session from 7.00 p.m. until 8.00 p.m. should remain the only official group. He said it would be wrong to set up rival times, and that this was a long established meeting that the regular five people who attended (out of the approximate congregation of eighty-five) were comfortable with. Rival times! Comfortable! This just about summed up the attitude of the church at times. How could other prayer groups be rivals? How could being comfortable be right when other people were not hearing the truth about God in a way that they could relate to?

Trenom made his views clear, but he felt like he was in the minority. The problem was that most church members seemed to think that non-Christians should be able to adapt quickly and easily to church culture, and if they couldn't, it was because they didn't really want to believe.

The whole issue of praying for the community had been lost amongst an underlying battle of control, power, and fear. Some members had high-flying careers and wanted that same power and control in the church. They tried to make it a smooth-running business. Others with dull existences outside of the church tried to find some kind of power by holding positions of authority in it. Obviously, there were a lot of good people within the membership who served the church, but the power crazy were rooted in self. Their opposition to ideas other than their own was subtle, but destructive.

All Trenom wanted was for the church to seek God to see if anything needed changing. But most people do not like change because it threatens their security.

What was agreed at the end was that people could pray informally over the issues raised as long as it didn't clash with the normal prayer group. It felt like a peace offering to keep Trenom quiet, and he thought that nothing was ever going to change.

After the meeting, quite a few people came to him to say that they agreed with him. This was encouraging, but why didn't they say anything in the meeting?

As Trenom prayed alone that night, he brought the people who had opposed his views before God. He didn't much feel like loving them, but he knew he had to, to avoid taking offence and becoming bitter.

Interest in the unofficial prayer group surprisingly grew over the next few weeks, and the prayers of those present were passionate and genuine. It seemed to be a move of God as people cried out to Him to change their own lives and to show them how to reach out to others.

Soon the minister was attending occasionally along with some of the other leaders, but one of these leaders stirred up negativity. He urged caution, and, of course, this was wise, but he also spread rumours that Trenom was trying to control the leadership. Trenom knew this wasn't true, and he also knew that opposition always comes to any work of God, even sometimes in its strongest form from within the church.

He had permission from the church to go ahead with these meetings, and so he was determined not to become discouraged. His prayers became bolder, and he passionately desired to find the heart of God.

There was no doubt that something was happening. The church was steadily becoming a people of prayer, and the prayers were full of honesty and warmth. There was no need for big or religious-sounding words. This was authentic spiritual desperation and a raging hunger from the hearts of God's people to find His will.

Some people at the church were just not interested in this prayer group, and the subtle opposition to undermine it continued. But the prayer carried on.

Trenom had asked anyone who prayed about the local community to write down any thoughts they had and to give the information to him. It was now nearly six months since the start of their seeking after God, so he decided to collate all the ideas he had been given, which ranged from a couple of lines on a scrap piece of paper to full-blown essays. As he searched through this assortment of common sense, crazy ideas, and he hoped, a lot of God's heart, a definite pattern was emerging. Trenom excitedly wrote up a summary and arranged to meet up with the minister of the church to share it.

As he approached the minister's office, he did so with trembling legs. He thought God had spoken, but it would mean some changes in the church, and that never went down well with some people. As he sat down, he was bombarded with negative thoughts that maybe this wasn't such a good idea. But after a few seconds of trying to compose himself, he went ahead despite his feelings.

Trenom began by saying that the ideas he was going to share were not necessarily God's plans for the church. He just wanted the vicar to pray and test the ideas with God to see if any of them were right.

The first point he made to the minister was that there had been an overwhelming viewpoint that the church needed to get away from busyness. They had been involved in so much that the most important thing, a personal and intimate relationship with God, had been stifled. *Doing* things for God had become more of a priority than *being* with Him. Trenom knew that the minister was involved in a lot of activities. If there had been a committee that organised committees, he would have been chairman. He hoped he wouldn't take it personally. He still *seemed* to be listening.

Trenom also mentioned that it might be a good idea to review all of the church's activities, to perhaps even temporarily stop everything, to seek God's heart and test what He wanted them to be involved in.

Another idea raised by numerous people was that more friendship and special interest groups could have an important role in reaching out into the community. Trenom explained to the minister that he originally thought that this contradicted his first point, as it seemed to be adding extra church busyness, but he now believed that this would not be the case. If the church suspended its schedule and then spent time seeking to be involved in only God-led activities, it would hopefully lead to a healthy, fruitful busyness. It would also remove the pressure of being an activity-based church, where guilt is put upon the congregation if they are not busy enough. This wasn't an excuse for laziness. If people were intimate with God, out of that would come activity, and it would be Godly activity.

Friendship groups were nothing staggeringly original. The aim of these groups though had always been to eventually lead people into the main Sunday service, where many people felt disconnected. Church culture sometimes bored the new and old Christians to death. If they'd had any kind of passion, excitement, or sense of adventure, they were in danger of having it put on death row before it was given a lethal injection by someone wearing a grey mask of false respectability. Then after having their heart wounded and crushed, they would either disappear or put on their own grey mask, as the colour drained from their unique personalities. There were some lovely people in this church, but sometimes 'all-age worship' could be more appropriately renamed 'most-age irrelevance'.

Trenom suggested that a change of focus could be a possibility, and he proceeded to explain his idea, although he knew that the minister would probably disagree with it. He stated that if the pressure to mould people into church culture was taken away and the emphasis shifted to helping people into a relationship with God in ways and styles that reflected their own personalities and talents, it would encourage Godly diversity and freedom, rather than binding everyone up in aspects of church culture that were unnecessary. Obviously, Christians needed to meet and share together, but maybe the whole way of doing this needed to change for the vast majority of people to be able to seek God in a real way. Trenom had a lot more to say, but paused, waiting for a reaction from the minister. After an awkward few seconds of silence, the minister frowned, stroked his chin, and asked for some practical suggestions.

Trenom forged ahead. He stated that if the church spent time in real intimacy with God, as he had already mentioned, with the idea of starting more friendship groups, people may be prompted by God with specific ideas. If the church leadership tested this, and there were enough people willing to work in a team, friendship groups and special interest groups could be started and advertised to the community. There could be art and design groups, food groups, or any other group where people had a common interest or hobby. They could be run in the name of the church by a group of Christian leaders who were accountable to the church. There wouldn't be any preaching involved, but each group would adhere to Christian principles.

It would be good, from time to time, if there were opportunities to explore spirituality by including a spiritual aspect in the normal group. For example, it would probably be easy and non-threatening for a design group to explore spirituality. There would be no pressure on people to attend anything other than their own friendship group, and they would still be genuinely welcome even if they expressed no interest in anything spiritual. These ways of exploring spirituality would be relevant to each group. They would not be based on giving people all the answers but on listening to other people's views and their spiritual journeys.

The minister had raised his eyebrows at the word *spirituality* and was concerned that this was going to be a pick and mix type of religion that watered down the truth of the gospel. He quizzed Trenom on exactly what he meant.

Trenom explained that the leaders and Christians at each group would share the truth of the gospel at times of spiritual discussion, whether this was a natural opportunity at the friendship group or an arranged extra meeting, but they wouldn't just preach it via a pre-packaged series that failed to listen to others' life stories. Another important factor would be that other peoples' locations on their respective spiritual journeys would not be condemned. The gospel message was obviously truth in Trenom's opinion, and absolute truth surely meant that Christians didn't have to be defensive or insecure about others' beliefs or non-beliefs.

It would be made clear from the start that each activity was being run by the church, but there wouldn't be a hidden agenda, just people enjoying their interests, using their gifts, and building good relationships. The church would pray that God would use these friendship groups to reveal Himself, and Christianity could then be explored in more detail at the Godly appointed time. Maybe some other church groups could join together for this when it was relevant to them and would promote understanding. When anyone became a Christian, there would be no pressure to attend the Sunday morning service, although they could. They would be mentored in their friendship group, which would be a much more intimate setting and promote growth in a natural way.

The minister was still listening.

Trenom explained that one of his ideas for the football team was to have a camping trip at a local beauty spot and to discuss the vastness of the universe around the campfire and under the stars. This would be a totally non-threatening and inclusive way of exploring spirituality. There could then be other more specific ways of looking at Christianity for those that were interested, in a relevant style of learning and exploration for that specific group. Again, this would look at the truth of the gospel, but not in an aggressive or insecure manner.

Trenom stated that he felt the church needed to get away from its obsession with trying to get all people with any connection to the church, ultimately, to attend the traditional Sunday service. In Trenom's opinion, this one-service-fits-all way of doing church didn't increase unity; it hindered it and stifled church growth as people became frustrated and alienated. Many people who had an interest in God just couldn't relate to church.

Leaders of church activities, such as the football club, made good relationships and saw some genuine spiritual interest from others. They then tried to explain the principles of the Christian faith in a way that was relevant for that group. However, a lot of these seekers then didn't want to go to church or went occasionally but soon lost interest.

This resulted in some group leaders keeping their group almost completely separate from the church. Then no one else in the fellowship really knew what was happening. It also left those leaders with a sense of guilt and failure as they couldn't do what the church required of them, which was to give people the opportunity to hear about God and then lead them into church.

If this focus changed and people were allowed to search further at their own speed and within their own friendship group, it would surely be a good thing. The group could then expand for those who were interested, and they could discover truth and grow in faith within a context that was relevant and without the pressure of having to wear the debilitating church culture body armour which weighs so much and can destroy diversity and creativity.

The minister interrupted at this moment and raised some concerns. He was worried that Trenom's ideas would cause the church to become fragmented and cease to be a body, as it appeared that the church would never meet together.

The minister's comment was perfect timing as it led right into Trenom's next point. He wasn't stating that the main Sunday service should be cancelled. Some people were able to relate and worship in that traditional way. But there should not be such importance placed on attendance defining your faith.

As for the church being fragmented, this was already the case. There were regular church attendees but very few new people from the fringe groups such as parent and toddler or the youth group. The body was disjointed. Some people only went to the main service out of a sense of duty or loyalty, and many were disillusioned.

This church didn't have a lot of unity and didn't act as a body, even if the smokescreen of getting everyone inside one building fooled some people. There had to be a way of getting the people of God to meet together though, and Trenom said that he was getting to that point as he saw the colour disappear from the minister's cheeks.

He explained that to encourage unity and to work as a body, all the Christians from the separate groups could meet, perhaps once a month, to spend time together. One group could possibly cook a meal for the others, and another could share what had been happening in their group. Or perhaps they could all do something for someone who needed help in the local area. Prayer for God's work in each of the groups would be an important part of this meeting together, but it would be a relaxed and informal time of encouragement. Ideally, there would be no pride or competition amongst the different groups and an acceptance from everyone that people could worship in many different ways and places but still come together as one body to encourage each other in their different ministries in an authentic unity.

There could also be events arranged where everyone at each friendship group was invited, whether they were a Christian or not, as long as this was prayed through and organised with Godly wisdom. All the annoying things about church culture would hopefully be absent. Icebreakers, words that no one uses anymore, and silly false smiles would be locked up in a time capsule, covered in a patterned cardigan, and buried in the organ.

Trenom thought that he had communicated all that he wanted to say and exhaled a long quiet breath as he leant back into his chair, put his arms around the back of his head, and waited for a response.

His ideas were not dismissed immediately. The minister said he wanted some time to think and pray about what they had discussed. This was obviously a wise and correct reply, but it could have been a way of avoiding the issue. Trenom hoped the issues would be genuinely and prayerfully considered.

6.

Opposed Breakthrough

Trenom was slightly nervous as he listened to his answer phone and heard the voice of the church minister asking him to return his call. It had been a while since their conversation, and Trenom presumed that he was ringing to gently reject his ideas.

Trenom returned the call, and to his amazement, the minister said he had thought and prayed about their conversation, and he felt that God was leading them into some of the ideas that Trenom had talked about. The ideas would need some careful, wise, and sensitive planning, but he felt that God was leading them into something new. The minister also revealed that he had shared these thoughts with the other members of the leadership team, some of whom opposed them. He was going to arrange an urgent special meeting with all of the church to discuss the matter further.

Trenom was jubilant, and straight away he prayed that God would intervene and that His will would be done. If the ideas were not right, he wanted God to block them, but if they were right, he prayed that God would lead the church in making changes despite opposition.

Trenom presented his views for change at the church members' meeting, and as he finished, those assembled were silent as they thought through the matter. The minister asked for opinions, but the assembly remained quiet for a while. This was an apathetic silence that can appear whenever change is proposed. People seemed happy to keep on doing things the way they had always done, even if they saw no real signs of growth.

One of the church leadership team broke the silence and spoke out.

'These ideas are a disgrace and would dishonour God, as the church would devolve into a social club for people who just want to enjoy themselves,' he said angrily.

'The effectiveness and unity of the church body will be damaged, and the sanctity of the church service will be lost,' added another leader, in an agitated tone.

There were also numerous comments about the importance of attendance at the main church service and that all people should adapt to the status quo.

The new ideas were crumbling under the hymn singers and traditionalists. Trenom was beginning to think he had got it wrong, but he also realized that pride motivated those who wanted to keep things the same, and they were willing to exclude many people unless those people conformed to something totally irrelevant to them.

Trenom wanted a chance to answer some of the negative comments, so he did.

'The idea of the church becoming a social club isn't what I had in mind, but that description isn't all bad. Surely community and belonging are important principals in the kingdom of God,' he said. 'A believer doesn't have to be miserable all the time and not enjoy the company of others. Of course, having fun isn't the main purpose of church, but if changes were rooted in an intimacy with God and the church was involved in the diversity of real life, this would surely lead to the growth of God's kingdom,' he continued, in an exasperated tone.

Trenom then repeated what he had said to the minister about unity.

'Having a full house in one church service does not necessarily mean that there is unity or that the body of the church is working effectively. If the people of the church could use their gifts and interests without the pressure to conform to aspects of church culture they find unhelpful, then apart from benefiting their own relationship with God, these changes would make the true gospel message much more accessible to church members' school friends and work colleagues and the local community as a whole. At the moment, some people feel embarrassed to bring anyone along to church services or activities.'

Trenom reiterated that he wasn't saying that the Sunday church service should stop. He appreciated the fact that some people liked the current way of worshipping, and the service could be a type of friendship group for them. But he thought that one style of worship shouldn't define everyone's faith. He suggested that if everyone met occasionally in a less formal manner for a particular task or event, then that would be a far better way to bring about unity. It would also help the church body function in a healthier way.

The comment about people having to fit into the way church was presently done had particularly irritated Trenom, and he expressed his frustrations.

'Church services are just not relevant for a lot of spiritual searchers. Something has got to change,' he said passionately.

Exhausted, Trenom sat down. Another short period of silence followed, but ended when some of those in attendance made positive comments about his ideas. Some members were at last either finding the bravery to speak out or beginning to understand the vision.

A lot of people expressed their concern about inviting their friends to informal church activities, as, in reality, they were wrapped up in a church culture that outsiders found hard to relate to. Church events always ended with some kind of spoken message, preached like a lecture that often left people feeling as though they were being told off. Listeners had no trust or relationship invested in the speaker and they had no opportunity for interaction.

It seemed that this presentation of the gospel rarely brought any new people into a relationship with God or into the church. Was this because people just didn't want to know about God, or was it because the context it was presented in was largely irrelevant to them? If it was the latter, then surely something needed to change, and some of the church members now seemed to appreciate this.

Church members discussed many other negative and positive points before the minister eventually called a halt. He thanked the members for their input and expressed his opinion that changes should take place.

The church required a certain percentage of members to be in agreement to go forward with any proposal, so the minister put the matter to a written vote scheduled for a month hence, giving people enough time to think and pray about it.

During the next few weeks some church members tried to persuade others of the possible negative consequences of any changes. Was the church moving away from the truth? Would the changes lead to chaos, making members unaccountable to the leadership? Were people going to be forced to be involved with activities that they didn't want to be a part of?

It was a tough time for Trenom. Some people spoke to him with words that were dressed in Christian metaphors that on the surface seemed to be godly and helpful. However, these words masked disagreement and discouragement and were aimed at putting a stop to any changes. Although some of the remarks may have been caused by genuine caution, most were based on selfishness and fear. The people who were doubtful about changes were in favour of what *they* liked or felt comfortable with, and they didn't seem to communicate anything from the heart of God. Trenom returned to God in prayer. If God wanted changes to happen, he prayed that they would go ahead.

As the church met for the vote, debate continued, but the minister brought the meeting to order and asked that the voting slips be handed out. After the church secretary and other officials collected and counted the votes, the minister confirmed that the changes would be implemented. The church would begin changing its focus to friendship groups.

Two of the leadership team resigned immediately. Other church members shouted that they intended to leave the church and stormed out of the meeting.

Trenom was devastated. He had only presented what he thought God was saying to him. His ideas had caused a rift in the church, and that didn't feel good.

After the meeting, the minister, looking drained himself, tried to encourage Trenom. He knew they would have a tough time ahead, but he agreed that they were doing what God wanted. They needed to move forward, but they also needed to deal with any opposition in a godly way.

A number of people did in fact leave the church, and there was some gossip in the community about the church falling out with each other. Trenom was plagued with thoughts that he had caused all of this and that he had possibly damaged the church's chances of sharing the truth about God with the community.

The minister continued to be a real encouragement to Trenom and the rest of the congregation. Despite the fact that they were broken in many ways, he pulled them together, and they began to experience real intimacy with God. Many activities within the church stopped, particularly those that didn't have enough leaders and helpers, and although this was unpopular with some people, it made spending time seeking God a priority. The people left in the congregation truly united. They were now a church that was spending more time listening to God and less time involved in loads of activities.

Of course, there was work to be done, and after seeking the heart of God for many months, ideas started to surface from church members with suggestions of possible friendship groups. Some members still thought that the church should be involved in more activity and that doing less was a sign of laziness. But the place seemed much healthier, and the worship and awe of God seemed to deepen. New activities began only after much prayer and testing and with a structure of trained leaders. The leadership team for any activity led because of a calling from God, not just because they sensed a need. This changed the whole emphasis of serving, and it took away the spirit of guilt that had been so prevalent amongst those not involved in church activities in every spare moment. There was a new freedom now. Church members could just spend time with God, waiting for his prompting and relying on His power, rather than becoming exhausted by busyness.

Some people seemed to come alive after years of feeling guilty or stifled. They were serving God out of a love for Him and were allowed to show that love through their own interests and personalities in new groups.

One such group was an after-school club held at the local primary school. For many years the numbers at the church Sunday school had been declining, and now only three children attended regularly. The age difference between them was large, and it was impossible to teach a programme appropriate to each of their needs. A leaflet drop around the town to advertise the Sunday school had failed to bring any new children into the church, but the new after-school club had a waiting list within days. The club had leaders who were trained by the church and then released into service. They led art, drama, sport and other activities emphasising Christian principles, although they weren't allowed to present an overtly Christian epilogue in the new programme.

Trenom felt that a burden had been lifted from him as he continued his own role working with the football team. He had always felt under pressure to ensure that some of the players came to Sunday morning church service, and he felt guilty when they didn't. Now that the definition of church was different at the congregation, Trenom no longer felt a legalistic bondage, and he had the freedom to be the person God had created him to be. He wanted to share the gospel, and he knew that this had to be done through the power of God, and not according to some six-point plan or manufactured product. As far as Trenom was concerned, the gospel message could be proclaimed most effectively after you had been involved in someone's life, loved them and listened for God's prompting.

One thing that Trenom organised was a camping trip for the football team. It had been on his mind to arrange something like this for a while, and at last it was going to happen. The team already felt a real sense of community and belonging, and Trenom wanted to strengthen their bond. He had planned for the trip to happen just before the start of the new football season, and various groups at church offered much prayer to God, asking Him to reveal something of Himself to the team.

7.

Journeying with Integrity

Cheraser was excited, as the first night of pre-season training had arrived. He had been at the football club for eighteen months now, and he was enjoying it. He still didn't show much emotion, but he had a great respect for the team and for Trenom in particular. He had kept away from all church activities since his bad experience at a service, but Trenom never pressured anyone into attending anything, and Cheraser trusted the leadership of the club and enjoyed being around them.

Tonight's weather was hot and sticky, and the training was difficult. As the session ended, the players collapsed onto the floor and drank any water that they could find. As normal, only a few people had brought a drink with them; their bottles were passed around and then returned with just the dregs left in the bottom.

A weekend camping trip for the team was coming up before the football season started. After Cheraser had been convinced that this wouldn't be used as an excuse to preach at him for two days, he wanted to go. Most of the team would be there, and it seemed like it would be a good laugh and a time to bond.

As the day of the trip arrived, Cheraser packed his things and crammed them into the back of the hired minibus, ready to make the short journey to the campsite. He was sharing a tent with a couple of the other players, and after they had erected it in the most complicated way possible, they joined the rest of the team for a barbeque.

It was a relaxing evening with lots of food, chatting and a few beers. As the sun started to set, the beauty of the surroundings suddenly revealed itself. The campsite looked out onto some hills, and the only noise was the sound of birds and the odd vehicle in the distance. It was hard for them to believe they were only a few miles from a busy town.

Something touched Cheraser in a spiritual way, and he started up a conversation about the vastness of the universe and the meaning of life. This was too much for some players, who drifted off to their tents. Others just fell asleep where they were lying, but a few joined in the discussion with their opinions about the world.

'I believe in a creator who loves and cares for us,' said Trenom.

'As I look around, the creator theory makes some sense,' replied Cheraser. 'But all the crazy bad things that happen in this world seem to either rule that theory out, or mean that the creator is cold and impersonal,' he continued.

The creator Trenom talked about seemed like a loving father, but at the moment, Cheraser couldn't see that. It was a great conversation, however, and everyone was allowed to have their own opinion without being shouted down.

As everyone settled down for the night, Cheraser spent some time on his own, just staring at the stars. The number seemed to be limitless. He decided that if there was a creator, he wanted to know about Him. His opinion of God had, until now, been of a fun-spoiling, rule-making, boring, irrelevant being, and that was reinforced by his experience of church. But if there was a God that made the universe, then the reality was very different. This was not someone you could describe in a rational way and package up in a box. It was someone who was so awesome that the human mind could not totally process who he was.

Cheraser still couldn't understand how a creator could allow so much bad stuff to happen in this world, but maybe something had happened to spoil it. The natural beauty surrounding the campsite did seem to cry out, 'I have been created, and what you see is the evidence. I am not here because of some random physical phenomena.'

Cheraser was determined to explore the possibility of a creator, and this increased his already fierce hunger for spirituality.

He had a great weekend, and it was good to take time out to relax and think about something bigger than himself. He liked the fact that people had listened to his opinions. The church people amongst the team hadn't judged him or preached at him, but neither had they diluted what they themselves believed in. The care their actions showed spoke to him more than anything they said.

As he got back home, he felt very flat. Being part of a community for the weekend had touched something deep within him, and now that had ended.

A familiar face was quick to the scene to heal the hurt inside.

'Cheraser, my friend, I can make you feel better,' said Stul, and she rolled her tongue slowly over her top front teeth. 'Just look at a few pictures on the Internet. They are your friends as well.'

Cheraser's heart started to beat quickly, and he stared at her beautiful face for a couple of seconds as she stood seductively on the pathway. That was always enough time for him to be convinced, and he used a key that she had given him some time ago to unlock the chain on one of her crosses. He then quickly walked through the doorway.

Internet pornography always gave Cheraser an escape from reality and took away any pain he was feeling, at least for a while. It was like receiving a pleasurable sedative. Later, Cheraser crashed on his bed.

The pathway was a stunning sight. Elaborately carved crosses coated with sparkling jewels were all around, and they each seemed to have a power that drew Cheraser towards the door. The crosses, though, seemed to have something missing, but as Cheraser tried to work out what this was, his thoughts were interrupted by a trustworthy voice.

'There is nothing missing from the crosses; you just need to let the keyholders unlock the chains around each one and go find peace and fulfilment,' said Slafe convincingly. 'You can see that there is beauty and wonder on this pathway, but just accept it. Don't try to think of a creator. It is not healthy and will disturb your mind. Just enjoy the pleasure of the moment,' added Slafe.

As the words sunk in, Cheraser accepted them as truth.

'I'll let you in on a secret,' said Slafe. 'If you keep opening chains to deeper and deeper crosses, you will find a great reward when you eventually get to the end of the journey.'

Cheraser quickly entered a doorway to a cross that Slafe himself had unlocked.

Cheraser concluded that maybe he should stop thinking so deeply. There were lots of opportunities in this life, and he just wanted to enjoy himself. Maybe true happiness just amounted to making good choices and getting what you could out of life.

At the next football training session, all the talk was about the camping trip. It had certainly brought the team together.

'After some of the conversations that we had on the trip, I am considering starting up a group at my house to discuss spirituality,' said Trenom, speaking to the squad of players during a break in training. 'This will come from a Christian viewpoint, but it will not be preachy and will allow people to be honest about what they believe without being judged. There will be food and drink, and it will hopefully continue the sense of community that was so tangible when we were camping,' he continued.

'I would definitely be interested,' said Cheraser. He surprised himself that the words came out of his mouth so quickly. He immediately felt a bit embarrassed and hoped that he wasn't the only one who had a desire to attend. He didn't want to be seen as a religious freak. Thankfully, a few others did eventually show some positive interest, which was unusual. Mention of any activity connected with the church was normally greeted with an embarrassing silence.

Cheraser's desire to learn about spiritual matters seemed to change daily. At times he was excited at the prospect of discovering truth, but on other occasions he was apathetic towards the possibility of a deeper meaning. The chance to discuss more on the subject had re-ignited his enthusiasm though. There was enough interest to make a viable group and it was arranged that the first meeting would take place after training next week.

Over the following few days, Cheraser began to regret saying that he would attend. After football training and maybe a quick drink at the leisure centre bar, he just liked to go home and relax in front of the television with a takeaway.

> Treger joined Cheraser on the pathway.
>
> 'You shouldn't have said you would go. You don't need it. There will be a tense atmosphere, and you shouldn't be there,' said Treger in a disappointed tone.

Cheraser didn't want to miss training, but he had every intention of making up some excuse to avoid going to Trenom's house afterwards. However, when training had finished, he didn't want to disappoint anyone and decided to go along.

The evening was actually much better than Cheraser had expected. People from the church had cooked some good food, and the atmosphere was great. Trenom led a small discussion time, and there were some good conversations. Everyone was given the chance to voice an opinion if they wanted to. One quieter person from the team felt relaxed enough just to lie on the floor and listen. The evening flowed in a natural way. Quite a few personal issues were raised, and although Cheraser didn't really understand some of the spiritual beliefs that people had, he appreciated the fact that he could share his views and ask questions.

What challenged him most after a few weeks of these discussions was not what was said, but how people from the church had acted. Why had they taken time out to cook for him or be interested in him? They seemed to accept him as he was, and they also seemed to be passionate about this God that they worshipped in a way that contained vitality and humility.

The time spent around the Christians in this football team had started to affect Cheraser in a deep way, and he wanted what they had. It wasn't religion or being nice or good. For them, it was about a relationship with someone who had created them and the world that they lived in.

Cheraser, though, despite his experiences could still only see God as an impersonal being. His thoughts about God crashed against each other, causing confusion, but also leading Cheraser to search for the truth.

He continued to ask questions in the laid-back surroundings of Trenom's house, alongside people he had good relationships with and whose company he enjoyed. No one forcefully argued their case, but they were willing to explain their journey of faith, or non-faith, whilst listening to others' point of view.

After one particular evening at Trenom's, Cheraser pondered the meaning of life again.

> Cheraser was pulled onto the pathway by a group of strong, pushy men. They left him on his knees, with his mind spinning, and only the comforting voice of Slafe brought some welcome respite.
>
> 'Sorry that they were a bit rough, but you needed help,' said Slafe, sympathetically. 'Let me just remind you of all the good things in your life.'

Stul, Lutocc and Dreeg all appeared and dangled keys enticingly in front of Cheraser. Stul even danced in front of him, brushing her face against his.

Lutocc suggested that Cheraser should keep searching for more spiritual experiences and offered him a key to unlock a door to a room full of special helpers. They would guide him and enable him to have more knowledge and power.

Stul and Lutocc then walked away hand in hand, peering slyly over their shoulders and giving Cheraser the impression that he would miss out if he didn't take their advice.

As they disappeared, Dreeg put his arm around Cheraser, unlocked one of his own crosses, and gave him a glimpse of piles of money and a life of luxury before quickly re-locking the chain and disappearing.

Slafe was left on his own, staring at Cheraser, with his arms wide open, palms outstretched.

'You wouldn't want to miss out, would you? If you start believing in all of that God nonsense, you won't be able to do anything enjoyable, and you'll have to go to church. Do you remember how you hated that? You'll be a clone before you know it,' said Slafe, in a tone that bordered on sarcasm. He looked disappointedly at Cheraser, and then he was gone too.

Cheraser, feeling lonely and bewildered, didn't know how to get off the pathway, but he was quickly helped by Aref, who had suddenly arrived to lead him through the doorway to an already unlocked cross.

Cheraser saw something attractive in the Christian people he knew, but he was still wary of fully getting involved himself. He loved talking with them and asking questions, but it was all head knowledge. His spiritual exploration didn't require any moral changes, and he didn't want to change anything anyway as long as he could find real happiness. He certainly didn't want to attend church. He found it difficult to figure out the connection between the Christians he knew, who were passionate but still human, and the lifeless, irrelevant experience he had had of church. But he continued to ask questions at the weekly get-together at Trenom's house, and he even started to talk about spiritual matters before and after football matches or during training. He was truly searching for something, and he had one big question that he needed to have answered. If God did create the world and everything in it, and he cared about us, why was the world such a horrible place to live in sometimes?

Cheraser quizzed Trenom on this point, who answered by saying, 'In the beginning, God did create a perfect world. He also created the first man and woman and gave them some guidelines on what they could and could not do. These guidelines were not just for the sake of making rules; they were from a loving Father who wanted them to enjoy a perfect relationship with Him.' Trenom continued, 'But God didn't force them to obey; He gave them free will, as he didn't want to create robots. He wanted them to love Him and be in relationship with Him by choice. The first man and woman chose to be selfish, and at that moment their relationship with God was spoilt, and the world was no longer perfect.'

Cheraser was listening intently, and Trenom realised that his friend was ready to hear more. After a short pause, he said, 'As a result of this selfishness, pain and suffering entered the world, and everyone inherited a selfish nature and a spirit that was dead and separated from God. When you were conceived, your relationship with God was already broken, and you were stained with a mark of rebellion against your creator. God could have punished the human race for trying to live without Him, but instead He had a plan to rescue us. He chose to send His Son, Jesus, who, although not conceived of a human father, was still fully a human being. The plan was for Jesus to show us an example of how to live, and then, even though He had done nothing wrong, be killed as a punishment for our selfishness, to make it possible for us to be in relationship with God again.'

Cheraser pondered this answer. Basically, this would account for the clash between the beauty of creation and the suffering which was also present. God created us, gave us freedom, and then created a solution when He saw that we had messed it up. We could now choose to have a relationship with God again, if we wanted to, without having to do anything to earn it.

It was some story, and it had taught him what a Christian really was. It wasn't just about doing good things, singing old-fashioned songs, or being a servant to a list of fun-spoiling rules. It was about having friendship restored with God as was originally intended.

Cheraser had now worked out in his mind what it was all about. He kind of admired anyone with faith, although for him, the information was enough.

Many more thought-provoking discussions took place at Trenom’s house, and there was always respect for the views of others.

8.

A Choice to Make

As Cheraser lay in bed one night, he was kept awake by the noise of traffic from a busy road nearby.

There was an incredible sound of cheering and celebration, as thousands of people lined up along the side of the pathway, praising and bowing down to an unseen leader in the distance.

Lutocc and Stul soon leapt from the side of the track and greeted Cheraser. Their joy was infectious, and they jumped and danced around, hugging him. They grabbed him by the hand, and all three of them were soon running along the pathway at high speed.

As they progressed, there seemed to be a hierarchy of importance amongst the people in the crowd. Some appeared to be groundworkers. Each one of them held a small key, and they were celebrating without inhibition. They seemed to be in large groups, under the control of individuals who were carrying large clusters of keys. Then there appeared to be governing groups giving out orders to the workers but still finding time to join in the celebration. Their keys were much more ornate, and Cheraser had a sense somewhere deep within that these keys could open chains to large areas.

Cheraser ran farther along the pathway until his companions brought him to a halt. He was puzzled as to why they had stopped, but Lutocc brought his attention to a recess at the side of the path. They approached it and furtively peered through a slightly open door. Cheraser had a feeling that he shouldn't be looking in on this private area. Inside was another group of people, and from the small amount of conversation that Cheraser could actually hear, it appeared that they were the rulers of the governors. They seemed to be planning something with frenzied passion, and although the mood seemed jubilant, they had no time for celebration at the moment.

Cheraser was unsure about what was happening, but the cheerfulness of his two mates and the sound of celebration behind him made him feel secure. He was certain that Stul and Lutocc would soon explain this mix of worship and exhilaration. Lutocc and Stul now let go of Cheraser's hand and fell to their knees. They talked and sang in a language that seemed to convey complete devotion, but Cheraser had no idea who or what this adoration was for.

As Lutocc and Stul got back to their feet, they pushed Cheraser forward, and he got his first glimpse of the leader of this massive group of people. He was in the distance, and Cheraser couldn't see him clearly, but he could sense his staggering beauty and powerful authority. The leader encouraged his crowd of workers to praise him relentlessly, and he held his head back and waved worship proudly upon himself. He loved every shout of adoration, and each one made him gasp with pleasure and self-importance.

'This is Tansa,' said Lutocc, with a tone of great reverence.

'He is the king of this path and leads the way to truth, happiness and freedom,' added Stul.

Cheraser was suddenly aware of countless other individuals around him who were travelling along the same pathway. Like him, they seemed to be searching for something that would give them lasting satisfaction and a purpose for living. Tansa's workers had now left the side of the pathway and mingled with these travellers. They were urging everyone to look ahead and wait for Tansa's leading.

Tansa then held up his hand and asked his workers to be silent before starting to speak to the crowd in a language that Cheraser couldn't understand. Lutocc quietly informed Cheraser that it was a message for all those travelling on the pathway, and he would translate it for him.

'Let me show you what we are celebrating,' said Lutocc, interpreting. 'I have made it possible for all humans to tread upon this path. You now have the freedom to do whatever you want. If it feels good, it is good. All rules are finished with, and morality is what you want it to be. Help people, especially if it gets you something in return, but put yourself first. Remember that you are in charge of your own destiny. The many keyholders along this path are ready to unlock more doors to allow you to enter their crosses. I can give you whatever you want. Do you want to continue the journey?' added Lutocc, still relaying the message.

Cheraser was so much in awe of this beautiful figure that he was unable to speak. He just nodded, wide eyed.

Another group of Tansa's workers then came into view. They were carrying a large wooden cross, holding it up for all those journeying on the pathway to see. A dead person was nailed to the cross, and heavy chains had been wrapped around the body to bind it to the frame. It was barely recognisable as a human figure, such was the severity of the physical injuries.

'This man tried to close down this pathway and get you to join his own narrow and uncomfortable one,' Lutocc translated as Tansa continued.

'He tried to stop you from making your own choices and living as you pleased. He was a fun-spoiling, rule-making individual. He tried to crush pleasure, creativity and spirituality. I killed Him so that you could have freedom to follow your own desires,' said Lutocc, concluding the translation.

The noise of celebration and worship echoed around the pathway, and countless workers jumped and danced around the cross, shouting abuse at the dead man and praising Tansa for his victory. Tansa gazed proudly at his crowd of workers and the many people journeying on the pathway, and he appeared to crave ever-increasing amounts of worship.

Suddenly, there was a massive crash, and a cloud of thick dust enveloped the path, making it impossible to see anything. As the dust settled, Cheraser realised that something very mysterious had happened. The cross was now flat on the floor, and there was no longer a body on it. There was silence on the pathway, only broken by the sound of smashed chains falling onto the ground. Cheraser could only see as far as the cross. The dust cloud was progressing along the track, and he was unsure if anything still existed ahead.

As he walked closer to the cross, Cheraser became aware that the Christian guys from the football club, along with other people who he didn't know, were surrounding it. They were talking to someone Cheraser couldn't see. It was obvious from the tone of their voices that they all had a close relationship with this person, and they were asking Him to reveal the truth to Cheraser. As they continued, Cheraser inhaled the beautiful scent of sweet-smelling incense that rose from the hearts of these people to the person who was as yet unseen.[1]

Cheraser felt a mixture of surprise at seeing some of his friends on the pathway and confusion as to what was going on. His friends seemed to age slightly as they talked, as though the events were unfolding over a long period of time. But, paradoxically, they also seemed to be in a place that was somehow timeless, and Cheraser's brain couldn't fully process this apparent contradiction.

A fatherly voice then began speaking. 'I am going to show you what happened to the man who was once nailed to this cross,' said the voice. 'It is painful for me, and it will be for you, but I will comfort you,' he added tenderly.

Cheraser then felt a strong, gentle hand wrap around him, and he immediately felt a sense of protection, although he still couldn't see the face of this unknown helper.

As Cheraser looked at the cross, the man from before was thrown onto it. His already battered body fell onto the coarse wood, splintering His raw skin. His wrists were viciously nailed to the frame. His legs were pressed together, bent and twisted, and a nail was hammered through the heel of each foot. The cross was then raised into the air.

---

1 Based on Revelation 5:8, the Bible.

The man screamed in agony, and Cheraser had to turn away for a moment. As he looked back, the man's face was contorted because the torture was so severe. His skin was peeling off in large chunks, and His whole body looked like it had been spray-painted with blood.

Cheraser noticed that the man was carrying a globe-shaped object on His shoulders, full of absolute filth. He had a closer look, and then turned to vomit as the smell of the contents seeped through.

'This contains all the selfish acts that everyone has ever done. It is not just crimes such as murder, but also things like lying, greed and hatred,' said the fatherly voice, with pain penetrating each word.

Cheraser suddenly became aware that his own selfish way of living was very wrong.

'This man was punished because of me?' asked Cheraser with tears in his eyes.

'Yes,' said the voice gently.

The man on the cross then cried out some words, and His life slipped away. It had been a brutal, inhumane and utterly disgusting punishment.

'I cannot look,' said the fatherly voice, but He still cradled and comforted Cheraser, despite His own anguish. Cheraser had also turned away again, but as he looked back, he saw that the man on the cross was bound in chains, with the weight of the globe and its disgusting contents still on His shoulders. His face gave some indication of the terrible suffering and mental torture that He had endured, and the workers were celebrating and taunting Him.

After a period of time, the cross crashed down to the ground, and the man miraculously came back to life. The chains fell off, and He stood up and trampled over the cross. The taunts and celebrations of the masses were silenced.

'Who is that man?' asked Cheraser.

'He is my Son, who died and then overcame death so that you can have a restored relationship with me. My Son has paid the price for your selfishness. I stand with you now, longing for you to give your life to me, so that I can show you the purposes I created you for,' said the man in a tender, fatherly manner.

'What about all the people I have met on the pathway?' asked Cheraser.

'I created them all to help me carry out my work. Tansa, who is now their ruler, wanted worship for himself, and he and some of my other helpers rebelled against me. Their purpose is to prevent you from finding the truth and to keep you away from an eternal relationship with me,' said the voice.

Cheraser was now aware of the filthiness of his own selfishness and the fact that this separated him from his creator. He longed for their relationship to be healed, and he asked God to forgive him for the wrong things he had done. He wanted God to lead him into the right way of living.

Cheraser was now at the foot of the cross, and he started to walk over it. This cross was not impersonal, like the ones he had encountered previously on the pathway. It was stained with blood and human tissue, and there was heaviness in Cheraser's spirit, as if the world's selfishness had been left there, dealt with once and for all. Tears streamed down Cheraser's face as he knelt upon the cross, unable to continue walking over it. The weight of his own selfishness was pushing his body into the splintered wood, and it made further progress impossible.

The sound of footsteps coming from the other side of the cross caught Cheraser's attention. He opened his arms and, despite the shame and guilt that he felt, called out for help. He needed assistance to enable him to walk along the cross and reach whatever was on the other side.

'The load is impossible for you to carry,' said a gentle voice. 'Let me take it from you, and I will deal with it. We will leave it here forever.'

Cheraser wanted to do something to earn this act of grace, but there was nothing that this person wanted in return. As Cheraser gave permission for his heavy load to be left on the cross, it was added to an already foul-smelling pile. It was revolting, and the whole of Cheraser's body wretched in disgust. He turned away from the pile and felt immediate relief.

Cheraser was helped along the cross until he reached the top. He looked up and saw a brick wall blocking the pathway ahead. In the wall was a doorway with a chain wrapped around it. The chain suddenly fell off, and there was a gentle knock that came from the other side.[1] Cheraser pushed the door open, and he was greeted by such beauty and holiness that his brain could not completely process it. He could partly see three people, but paradoxically it seemed there was just one person. It was a breathtaking and indescribable moment that he somehow realized was eternally significant.

The person moved towards Cheraser, and in His hand, was a beautiful golden key. Cheraser felt a sudden heaviness in his eyes. As his eyelids closed, he heard the sound of the key turning in a lock, and he felt the sensation of something opening within him. A gentle breeze surrounded him, and he heard what sounded like the lid of a box being closed and then sealed. Something inside of Cheraser had been brought to life, and he fell in reverence, unable to control his praise and worship.

'Welcome, my child,' said God, and He held Cheraser like a loving father.

A host of angels then appeared and praised God with their whole being because Cheraser had entered into a relationship with his creator. The angels' songs were so holy that Cheraser couldn't comprehend the full meaning of their worship. If they sang forever, it would be totally justified, as this creator and saviour deserved eternal praise.

---

1 Based on Revelation 3:20, the Bible.

9.

Separate but Together

Cheraser had known intellectually what a Christian was for some time, but it had slowly become personal to him. He had now accepted God's offer of forgiveness and relationship and accepted Christianity as truth.

Cheraser was, though, concerned about some of the nonsense of church culture, and after telling a delighted Trenom that he had become a Christian, he talked about some of his fears.

'I don't want to be a clone or be turned into a Christian robot. I don't even own a grey cardigan, have trousers that are three inches too short, or have a desire to attend endless coffee mornings,' he said. 'Neither do I want to do silly actions or dances to strange songs.'

The God Cheraser had met couldn't be restricted to a few songs and a nicely packaged sermon. He was behind the beauty of creation and the mysteries of the universe. He was endless, and Cheraser was desperate to know more about Him and go through life in intimate relationship with Him. But he had a genuine fear that church would crush his natural sense of adventure and turn him into a nice but boring person.

> Cheraser immediately found himself on a new pathway. It was much narrower and steeper than the previous one, and looked like it would be a long, hard trudge to the end. At the side of the path, Slafe and Aref mocked Cheraser.
>
> 'What has he done? He's going to have a cardigan on before you know it, and all his mates will think he's weird,' said Aref, nastily.
>
> 'This pathway is wrong for you. Come back and join us on the true way to happiness,' added Slafe in a friendlier manner.

Trenom had often struggled with church culture himself, and he tried to ease Cheraser's fears.

'Being a Christian should not crush your personality, but give life to it. There have been some changes made to make church more accessible to all,' said Trenom.

'In what ways?' enquired Cheraser.

'We have started various different interest groups, such as the football club. Christian principles are a big part of the club as you know, and other church activities follow the same model and introduce the Christian message in ways that are relevant to them,' replied Trenom. 'It is essential though that Christians of all interests meet together, so that they can work effectively and support each other,' he added.

Cheraser looked a little worried, and Trenom, wanting to reassure him further, carried on talking. He said 'Going to the Sunday morning church service will not necessarily be the place where everyone gets together. There will be other ways of bringing an overall sense of unity.'

Cheraser didn't want to hear any details about that at the moment though, and he was happy to be looking at the basics of the Christian faith, during the weekly meeting at Trenom's house. The group still contained a lot of the football lads, but there were a few people who had also joined from other church-related groups. It wasn't a dry, packaged course, and as this was a young, generally sporty and laid-back group of people, the discussions reflected this.

The format of the night had changed slightly, but non-Christians from the football team still came. Some of them joined in, while others just chilled out or went to sleep.

Cheraser tried to keep away from any other church-related activities; but there was a meeting coming up shortly where all the smaller groups met together, at the church, on a Saturday night. It was aimed at Christians, although everyone from each group was invited, and he felt that he should probably go. He didn't really want to spend a night with a load of people he didn't know, but he could just talk to his football mates, so he decided that he would attend.

Cheraser wasn't sure what to expect, but he knew there would be a meal. He thought, because of his limited experience of church, that it would be something like quiche, salad, and a few hard bread rolls with too much butter on them, all being eaten in a draughty old church room. When he arrived at the church, the atmosphere was much better than he expected. The room had a warm feel to it, with low lighting, and the chairs looked comfortable. The room was set up like a restaurant, and someone had put a lot of effort into getting the ambience just right.

Normally at this type of event, some well-meaning person mixes groups up so that attendees can 'get to know everyone'. Cheraser hated this, particularly when he was eating. Food tended to either fall off his knife and fork, or he unintentionally spat some out after being asked an ill-timed question.

Tonight was different though. Each group was seated together, and the football group had their own table. This actually added to the large group's unity, making people feel relaxed and reinforcing their sense of belonging. The person who introduced the evening strengthened this feeling by acknowledging the diversity of the groups but stating the importance of overall unity to serve the purposes of God. This was done in a bold manner, but in a way that made any non-believers feel welcome. The set-up also allowed those attending to avoid hugging and grappling with total strangers or having to hide under a table to keep away from forced conversations.

Everything seemed to be going well until Cheraser realised that the church gardening club were hosting the evening. He thought he would have nothing in common with these people; he had no interest in gardening, and these people all looked a bit sad.

> Cheraser walked upon the new, narrow pathway. As he made some progress, he was greeted by a torrent of abuse.
>
> 'What are you doing with these church freaks? You have nothing in common with them,' said the familiar voice of Aref. 'Just switch off and don't get friendly with any of them. You don't want people to know that you hang around with gardeners, do you?' Aref then disappeared, his howls of laughter subsiding in the distance.

As Cheraser finished off his meal, his conscience was pricked, as the home-grown vegetables from the gardeners' group were delicious. The group were also acting as cooks and waiters and waitresses, in a humble, servant-like way.

> Cheraser heard the voice of his heavenly Father as he paused on the path.

‘Cheraser, my child, I have given many gifts and interests to my children. Some of them will be different to yours, but they have a purpose in my kingdom. Celebrate diversity, and although you may not relate to the interests of others or get on with some people, love them and pray for them, and remember that you are all part of my kingdom.’

After the meal, one of the gardeners gave a short talk on what was happening in his group. He avoided giving too much detail about the gardening itself but mentioned that it had opened up conversations about the wonder of creation. He also talked about the joy that he found in growing food and sharing it with everyone tonight. He then prayed for all the groups, and there was a real unity about the place as people with different interests came together.

After the short talk, Cheraser found chatting a little awkward, but he did talk with one of the gardeners. He didn’t have a lot in common with this person, but spiritually they were brothers. Cheraser now realised something about the importance of unity amongst Christians. This didn’t mean that everyone should be forced into a one-shaped mould that trapped them, stifling their God-given personality and gifts. It meant showing humility and servant-like love to fellow Christians, and encouraging, sharing and serving with them, for the common purpose of God’s kingdom.

Cheraser now knew Christians needed to meet together, even if in human terms they had little in the way of shared interests. This had always been a massive barrier for Cheraser, and his limited experiences of church people and church services had in some ways hidden the truth of the gospel message.

Cheraser had needed an authentic example of Christianity. He had found that firstly at the football club and again this evening.

He shivered at the thought that he had almost completely rejected Christianity because of all the silliness that went on at the service he had attended with Trenom. He was determined to try and be the same person in and out of church circles, and he knew he would have to change some of his lifestyle. Deep within himself, he now wanted to be an example of God’s loving nature to others in a way that avoided religious legalism.

Cheraser sat on the pathway and listened to Father God.

‘Cheraser, you are in relationship with me because my Son has made it possible. There is nothing you need to do to earn my love. I love you completely and unconditionally. Walk closely with me, and I will show you my plans for you, and these plans will prosper you, not harm you. Even if they are tough, just trust me,' whispered God in a gentle tone.[1]

---

1 Based on Jeremiah 29:11, the Bible.

10.

Old Habits

Cheraser loved being with his mates, and he was determined not to withdraw from them now that he was a Christian. In fact, he looked at them as if through new eyes. He had a longing for them to find what he had, but he was determined not to behave as if he was from a moral super planet. His mates had started to notice some changes in him though, and he took some stick for his new-found relationship with God.

Even though the banter was mostly good humoured, he was treated differently as everyone tried to work out what had happened to him. Some were suspicious, and others respectful. Sometimes people were quite vocal about finding out what he now believed, whilst others just wanted to completely avoid the subject and were distant towards him. Negative feelings fought inside Cheraser, as he felt like an outsider.

Cheraser wanted to live a life that was an example of God's character and make people ask questions about why he behaved the way he did, but at times he wasn't completely sure of how to behave. His feelings and learned behaviour had previously caused him to act almost on impulse, as if bypassing his free will. But now, some of his thoughts fought out an unseen battle of bare-knuckled fighting, where Cheraser needed to call upon the power of God to discern the right course of action. When he did discern the right thing to do, he still had the choice of how to act. It was a three-way battle consisting of his human nature, a spiritual enemy and God. God had already won the battle, but Cheraser was starting a lifelong journey of being changed into the likeness of Him. He knew God wanted to give him a purposeful life, but what was God's way in each area of his life? Could he ever be free from the selfishness that had always been a part of him? Could he let go of habits and areas of his life that seemed enjoyable but were actually not good for him?

Drinking alcohol and going to the pub were two issues he needed to consider.

> Cheraser reached a part of the path that had a simple wooden cross standing at one side. He was surprised to see that the chain was unlocked and hanging loose, unlike the secure locks on the old pathway. As he opened the door and looked inside, it led to a slightly twisted lane. It sloped downwards and looked a lot easier to walk upon than the one which he was now travelling on. In the distance, Cheraser heard the muffled sound of music with the beat of a bass drum, along with human laughter and shouting. The lane would provide a welcome break, and Cheraser stepped through the door of the cross, down a few steps and onto it. A Fatherly voice provided some wisdom.
>
> 'Cheraser, I created you to be around other people. Going out is good, but please remember that our relationship is a priority. If anything becomes more important than that or damages it, it would be better for you not to be involved in that. I want you to be an example of me to those around you. Remember, my plans are to prosper you,' said God in a voice soaked in genuine care.[1]
>
> A slight wind then blew towards Cheraser. Even though it was gentle, it felt uncomfortable to walk against. Cheraser stood still for a moment, and then the breeze carried him effortlessly back through the cross and to the narrow pathway. He didn't want to go back inside that cross again. For him, it wasn't right, and it had taken his eyes off the journey along the narrow path, which he now knew was the road to truth and fulfilment. As he looked back, he saw that the chain to the cross was still unlocked. He wanted to lock it up and throw away the key, but there was no key or keyholder to be seen. Cheraser didn't understand why the door had been left open, but he pressed on with his journey.

Cheraser had an inner feeling that some parts of his social life had to end. He remembered that the original pathway he had walked upon contained some things that were good, some that were bad and others that seemed neutral. This started to make more sense to him

---

1 Based on Jeremiah 29:11, the Bible.

now, as he thought that nightclubs fitted into the latter. Some Christians would be able to enjoy the nightclub scene without compromising their relationship with God. In fact, some would be called by God to be involved in that area of culture. But Cheraser knew that he needed to be finished with that part of his life. He needed too much to drink to have the confidence to go dancing, and he often acted in a way that he was not proud of when he sobered up.

He still liked a drink in moderation, but he tended to stay on at the pub instead of leaving with those who were heading off clubbing. This actually turned into a blessing after a few weeks, as the pub became a lot quieter later in the evening, and Cheraser made some deeper friendships with his mates who also stayed behind.

His personality wasn't being changed into a non-thinking, lifeless human shell. He was on a journey that was renewing the way that he thought and acted. He was finding freedom and life the way that God had intended.

The last few months had been a bit of a honeymoon period for Cheraser in his Christian life. He had a joy for living, a new love for others and a real purpose for his life. It had been difficult at times, but he could live with a bit of banter from his mates.

Unfortunately, Cheraser was now lying on his bed and feeling incredibly low. Revelation Football Club had just been beaten in a cup semi-final, and he was gutted at missing out on playing in his first-ever final. He hated losing big matches, and he always needed to find some comfort on a bad day like this. He wanted to have a few drinks but knew he would probably have too many and regret it in the morning, so he stayed at home. Instead of doing something constructive, he just dwelt on the game and felt sorry for himself. He eventually switched on his computer to try to numb his mind for a while.

> Cheraser could hear his own heavy footsteps labouring along the pathway.
>
> 'This journey is too hard for you—just look how steep the path is,' said a familiar voice. 'There is nothing but a long uphill struggle, and maybe this God of yours is all in your imagination. Why not just enjoy yourself, and let me comfort you,' added Stul's seductive voice from the side of the path.
>
> Cheraser remembered what a good friend she had been and saw how attractive she was. She pointed to her cross at

the side of the pathway, and Cheraser was drawn to it. The chain surrounding the doorway to the cross was already unlocked. This was helpful, because Cheraser seemed to have lost the keys he was once given by Stul and Lutocc, and Stul did not seem to possess any now.

Cheraser didn't need much persuasion, and he quickly entered Stul's cross. He breathed a sigh of relief, as it led to a downward path that seemed easy to walk upon, although it contained very little light. He could see many unlocked chains to crosses as he walked into deeper and darker territory. The gratification was instant, and Stul didn't miss out on an opportunity to remind Cheraser of the benefits of this pathway.

'You don't have to wait until you get to the end of the journey for rewards, like you do on the narrow path,' said Stul. 'The prize for completing the trek on that boring one doesn't exist anyway; it is a false promise. If you keep travelling further along this route, you will definitely find an incredible reward at the end. It will bring you true happiness and freedom, and you can have a great time on the way,' added Stul, before talking furtively to some people who appeared to be subordinate to her.

Stul seemed to have plenty of other business on her mind, and she left quickly, leaving Cheraser with the group of friendly and attractive people who had just arrived. It seemed as though they had been asked to comfort him and numb his pain, and Cheraser felt a sense of freedom and validation for a short while. But then the atmosphere changed, and the group of helpers started to insult him.

'God is finished with you; He won't forgive you now. This is the sin that is unforgivable,' said one of them with a voice of condemnation. They gathered near Cheraser as he fell to his knees in guilt and hopelessness. They held hands as they danced in celebration around him, sniggered and continued to hurl insults and accusations that added to his misery.

'Get over it! You're on your own now,' they shouted, and Cheraser accepted the words in a mixture of guilt and self-pity.

Cheraser turned off his computer in disgust. Until now, he hadn't looked at pornography since becoming a Christian, and he felt ashamed. He was out of relationship with his Father God, and it was a lonely and dark place to be.

11.

Falling from a Height

Cheraser cried out to God in what he thought was vain hope, asking to be rescued from his misery. He wanted forgiveness, and he wanted the relationship with his Father to be restored.

Suddenly, the cross that once contained the body of God's Son came crashing down, ending the celebrations of Stul's helpers. As light began to fill the pathway, the group scattered and cowered, trying to find some darkness.

'My child, you are forgiven,' said the tender voice of the Father. 'My Son's death was a once-and-for-all sacrifice, outside of time, that will always be enough for anything you have done or will do wrong. Come back into my presence on the narrow pathway,' He added.

As Cheraser accepted the gracious offer, the gentle breeze appeared again. The hands of his father carried him gently back onto the narrow pathway. As he looked back over his Father's shoulder, Cheraser saw that the chain to Stul's cross was still unlocked, and he wanted it to be secured so that it would be impossible for him to enter it again. He asked God to lock or remove this cross, but there was no reply.

The pathway was pretty barren, and as Cheraser turned a corner, a tree with gloriously coloured fruit was a welcome surprise. A gentle breeze swayed the branches, and the tree released a couple of pieces of perfectly ripe produce at Cheraser's feet. He sat, ate, and, feeling duly refreshed, pressed on with his journey.

Cheraser was determined not to look at any more pornography, because it spoilt his relationship with God. He now felt good, as his guilt and shame had been removed. The disappointment of losing the football game stayed with him for a few days, but an inner joy and peace had returned. Cheraser had a fresh desire to be in relationship with God. He realised that he needed to spend more time in His presence, talking to Him and reading His written word, the Bible. There always seemed to be other things to do though. Playing sport, going out, watching television, or surfing the Internet all seemed easier and more exciting than spending time with someone he could not physically see.

Cheraser did have the conviction to take some time out from his busy life, though.

> Cheraser felt the arms of his unseen Father God wrap around his body like two strong but soft wings and carry him effortlessly along. There was also a comforting, warm breeze blowing from behind, which seemed to speed up their journey.
>
> They eventually came to a place where beautiful winged creatures stood holding simple wooden signs with immaculate writing carved into them. A cluster of small wooden crosses was situated behind each winged creature, and every cross had a door with an unlocked chain hanging from its handle.
>
> God carefully helped Cheraser to the ground and allowed him to read each sign. The first few were all carved with details of some of his own character traits. 'Tender heart', 'deep thinker' and 'adventurous' were all carved on individual signs held by the powerful-looking creatures. The effort that had gone into making them affirmed to Cheraser that he was valued by God.
>
> The next few signs he read were labelled with some of his interests, which included sport. He didn't feel he had any special gifts or talents, but as he looked at each sign, he felt a slight warm breeze run across his face.
>
> Cheraser also became aware of a lead seal that was being pulled effortlessly along the pathway by the gentle wind. It stopped at his feet. He picked it up, and he noticed that a message was impressed onto it. The message read 'God's possession. Eternal life guaranteed'.[1]

---

[1] Based on Ephesians 1:13–14, the Bible.

The seal appeared to be only a small part of something still to come, almost like a deposit, but it had boosted his trust in his Father. He also had awareness that however insignificant he thought he was, God wanted to use his gifts and personality for His purposes. In fact, they were originally from God anyway, and He wanted to refine them into His own likeness.

One thing that did confuse Cheraser though, was why there was a cluster of small crosses behind each winged creature. The crosses seemed to lead away from the narrow pathway, and Cheraser asked his Father what they were for.

'Cheraser, your gifts, personality and some of your interests are good, but only if they are used on the narrow pathway,' said the voice of God. 'For instance, when you are playing football, I can involve you in fulfilling my plans if you use the game as a form of worship to me and show my character to others. But if you worship the actual game of football and your own glory, then you have strayed through crosses that lead away from my purposes.'

Cheraser glanced once more at the signs that had affirmed him, and he never again wanted to enter a doorway to any of the counterfeit crosses. He called out to his Father God, asking Him to either lock the chains or destroy the crosses completely, but once again there was only silence.

Cheraser grasped the lead seal tightly to remind him that his future was secure and continued his journey.

Cheraser clicked off his online devotional guide and closed his Bible. It always seemed to be a real effort beforehand, but he now knew why he should discipline himself to spend time in relationship with God. He could once again put worries and problems into perspective and face them with God's help. He could also enjoy the good things in his life with a deeper, godly satisfaction.

He was starting to realise that eternal life started now, and that his whole existence should be about worshipping God. It excited him that some of his interests could be lived out passionately for his spiritual Father. He still needed changing in many ways, but his personality contained the very essence of God's character, and he was determined to let God change him into the person he was created to be. He saw a little more of the big picture of who God is, but this made him realise that the whole picture was even bigger than he could ever imagine.

Cheraser felt alive, and he was enthusiastic about the next all-together activity that the church was going to be involved in. The clubhouse and changing rooms that Revelation Football Club used were in a bad state. Lots of other clubs also used the facilities, but the local council was not prepared to spend any money on improving them. So the church had gotten permission to do some repairs and refurbishment. Loads of people got involved. A plumber and a carpenter who attended the church, aided by many willing amateurs with paint brushes and vacuum cleaners, spent the weekend turning it into something much more respectable and comfortable.

Afterwards, there was some simple barbeque food, and some of the football guys, including Cheraser, spoke about what was happening at the club and explained their team ethos. Even some of those from the church who didn't like football were able to share in this show of unity, and there was a big turnout from the players. It was encouraging that so many from the church and football club had supported the cause.

Cheraser felt a sense of accomplishment at a job well done, and after most people had left, he surveyed the work with Trenom and some of the other football lads. The sense of community and ownership had increased, and as they excitedly talked about the improvements, Cheraser's mind wandered.

> He was amazed to see that the once narrow, difficult path had led to a mountaintop. He was now looking out onto a breathtaking view of creation. There were other mountains in the distance, some with snow-covered tops, glistening as the sun rebounded off them. He could see animals grazing and streams of water flowing all around. This would all have fitted into the palm of God's hand, and there would still have been room to place infinitely more. It was mind blowing.

Trenom gave Cheraser a lift home, and as he got out of the car, he felt immediate loneliness and discouragement. It had been a great day, but now he was on his own.

> Cheraser was no longer on the mountaintop. Instead, he was on a slight downward track that was dusty and barren, and he soon forgot the blissful surroundings that he had been so in awe of earlier.
>
> The emptiness within intensified, and when he saw a smiling, familiar face, sat just ahead in the middle of the

pathway, he rushed forwards and sat down next to Stul. She put one of her hands on his shoulder and stroked his face gently with the other.

'Cheraser, you need some comforting,' she said seductively. 'Why don't you come through the doorway to my cross again? You know it will make you feel nice. Don't believe the empty promises of your so-called Father. What loving person would give you such good feelings, and then replace them with such bad ones?' she added accusingly.

Cheraser dwelt on the advice and went through the doorway of Stul's cross. He felt immediate gratification. He continued to enter more doorways to crosses that led to greater depths, which contained areas with ever-decreasing light.

The pathway was satisfying, for the moment anyway, but Cheraser didn't feel completely comfortable, and he halted his journey to consider whether he should continue. Immediately, he heard howls of raucous laughter approaching with increasing volume. Stul's helpers once again surrounded Cheraser, shouting abuse and accusations.

'You're not a proper Christian, and God wants nothing more to do with you. It is impossible for you to go back to the narrow pathway now,' shouted a ferocious voice.

Cheraser fell to his knees under the verbal onslaught, and, realising that he was in the wrong place, he pleaded with his Father to forgive and rescue him. The cross that once contained the body of God's Son came crashing down again, and light poured along the pathway, leaving Stul's helpers cowering and trembling.

The Father didn't expect Cheraser to make his own way back to the narrow pathway, and so He carried him until they reached it, and a gentle breeze eased them along.

Cheraser noticed a winged creature pointing to a recess at the side of the path. He entered nervously and stood open-mouthed at a tree that contained incredibly luscious-looking fruit. It was just out of reach, and his mouth salivated with desire. A gentle wind caressed the branches, and a couple of pieces of fruit dropped to the ground. Cheraser excitedly picked them up and ate them. He felt refreshed and began the journey again.

Cheraser was annoyed with himself. He had only recently spent time in the presence of God, and he felt that he had really met with Him and learnt new things about Him. But then, almost immediately, he had moved away from that relationship and back into his old ways. He had to continually battle with thoughts of shame and guilt, but eventually he found his joy and peace had returned as he let God deal with his wrong actions.

He was back on track and determined not to move away from being in right relationship with God. He knew being a Christian was about God's unconditional forgiveness and that he couldn't earn his way into a relationship with his spiritual Father, but in some ways he still tried to earn His favour. Cheraser started to keep a diary of how long it had been since he last looked at pornography, which was in some ways a good thing. But as days and then weeks of successful avoidance went by, he began to feel a sense of pride. He was sure he had fully beaten his habit.

12.

A Sickening View

There was a town fete, and the church had a refreshments stall. Cheraser hadn't been involved with the organisation of it, but how hard could serving drinks be? He turned up to offer his help and support.

As he arrived, he felt an immediate sense of embarrassment alongside a feeling of guilt for being embarrassed. There was a massive tent with a huge sign saying 'Prayer Tent' and a big wooden frame with some cheap paper stapled to it. Various Bible verses had been scrawled untidily onto the paper with an array of garish, fluorescent marker pens. Cheraser sensed a lack of sincerity and an underlying pressure that getting numbers into the prayer tent was probably the main priority of the day. There was also a tangible feeling of tension as helpers fought to be in control. The question of who should add milk and sugar to the tea and how an infinite number of fairy and sponge cakes should be laid out seemed to be important issues. Cheraser guessed there was probably a book under one of the tables to keep a record of how many people each helper had led, or forced, into the prayer tent. Maybe there was even a prize, something like a fusty two-hundred-year-old hymnbook, to be given to the person who ushered the most people into the tent or handed out the record number of flyers about Christianity.

Cheraser knew that the people from the church were trying to communicate the truth, so maybe he was wrong for being embarrassed. Possibly someone would welcome a chance to be prayed for, and maybe God would use words from the Bible to talk to someone, but it just didn't seem natural. It was probably important that people were aware that the church was in charge of the stall, but why couldn't they just serve and look out for God's leading when the opportunity arose? As the day went on, it seemed as though people bought a drink, looked on suspiciously at the tent, and avoided what seemed to be irrelevant. Cheraser had a walk around the fete and looked at the church stall from the outside. He sensed a slightly pious attitude and an overbearing effort to try to tell people about God. Again, they meant well, but it seemed this was being done out of a sense of duty, rather than being led by the Spirit of God and His timing.

At the end of the day, there had been no visitors to the prayer tent, and there were conversations amongst the helpers about what a godless society they lived in.

Cheraser knew that he would never have entered the prayer tent during his search for God, and a lot of genuine seekers probably wouldn't have either.

Although Revelation Church had seen some drastic changes, there were still some members of the congregation who were stuck in a time warp. Their attempts to share their faith, although well meaning, sometimes alienated the very people they were trying to communicate with. Old ways of sharing the Christian message were still valid in certain niche areas. But most people were unable to understand what the real truth was because the message was coming from an old-fashioned sub-culture. It was as if they were being spoken to in a foreign language that they had studied reluctantly for a couple of years. They could probably understand little bits of the story, but most of it was unintelligible.

Cheraser was saddened that many people searching for something spiritual were often put off finding the one true God because they hadn't seen an example of a true, Spirit-filled Christian they were in long-term friendship with. Instead, Christianity had been reduced to fliers and events, rules and regulations, and someone with a placard at a protest complaining about some non-Christian event or lifestyle.

Obviously, relevance was important in communicating the truth to other people, but there was something else missing, and Cheraser pondered what that could be.

> As Cheraser took some small steps on the pathway, it seemed a lonelier journey than it had ever been, and he felt deep anguish. His heart felt as if it was almost breaking with pain, and he collapsed onto his knees.
>
> He heard some soft footsteps behind him, and he was effortlessly scooped up into the strong hands of his Father. Cheraser began to sob uncontrollably, and he moved his

head towards God's chest for more protection. As he did so, he could feel his Father's heartbeat against his ear, and he sensed that his own feeling of sadness was a small fragment of the pain that God was feeling. Cheraser kept his eyes closed, and he didn't know how much progress was being made along the pathway. All he was aware of was the rhythmical up-and-down movement that you feel when someone is carrying you, and he just wished that his Father would hold him until the end of the journey.

With a sense of disappointment, he felt his Father's feet stop moving, and Cheraser was lowered gently to the ground. They had come to another recess at the side of the path, and once again there was a tree within it, decorated with beautiful fruit. A gentle breeze then brushed against the branches, and some of the produce fell to the floor. It seemed that the fruit had been desperate for someone hungry to come along, so that it could sustain them. God picked up the fruit, peeled it, and lovingly fed it to Cheraser. The fruit was tender and good. The pain in Cheraser's heart was still there, but he now felt ready to continue the journey. The gentle footsteps of his Father moved towards the entrance of the recess, and He beckoned to him to leave. Cheraser wanted to be carried, but a loving smile and a gentle pat on the back assured him that it would be safe to continue walking.

As Cheraser lay relaxing on his bed, a few things had become clearer. He knew that the one thing sometimes missing from Christian people's lives, including his own, was a godly love. It was an attitude of the heart that focused on the real needs of others. Sometimes, he thought that Christian events were arranged because of a desire to be seen doing the right thing. Maybe these events were occasionally rooted in pride and fear and were basically selfish, rather than coming from a godly concern about other people's eternal future.

An emotional pain began to surface inside Cheraser for his friends and family who were not Christians. If they had visited today's refreshment stall, it would probably have reinforced their negative, stereotypical view of a Christian. It appeared to Cheraser that some Christians had subtle feelings of superiority and an ungodly sense of duty. Therefore, the gospel message was communicated not just irrelevantly, but also without love.

Cheraser was humbled by these thoughts. The people at the church who annoyed him had all been helping at the fete earlier in the day. But his heart was starting to be softened, and he was beginning to see them as God's unique creations. They, like him, were loved by God, and He had a purpose for their lives, whatever their interests, faults and weaknesses.

But Cheraser's thoughts also turned to one member of his own family, who basically just lived in his bedroom with mind-crushing music for company most nights of the week. He then reflected on one of his mates who was a nightclub doorman, and a genuinely decent bloke. God loved these people and was relevant to them, but would they enter a prayer tent at a fete or sing along to contemporary Christian music?

Of course, God himself was the only person who could actually convince people that He existed, and He could do that in any way He liked. But Cheraser knew God used humans in His plans, and they needed to search His heart deeply, with the help of His Spirit.

Cheraser was glad that he had found Christians who had been willing to get alongside him without any agenda in a way that was relevant to him. They hadn't watered down their beliefs, but neither had they forced upon him aspects of church culture which were unhelpful. They had given him an example of God's character, and then allowed God to reveal Himself.

Cheraser realised that the church he belonged to had adapted in many ways and had changed into a community that made it possible for him to integrate with other Christian people. But some of the stuff that went on in Christian circles just didn't make sense to him. Maybe that was because of the diversity of others people's worship preferences, which Cheraser now respected as valid and true. But sometimes it seemed that the church only related to middle-class people, who liked singing, flower arranging or monthly group breakfasts.

The Christian message was often shared in a way that was relevant to only a few. This drained the life out of its true meaning, reducing it to a man-made lifestyle and set of rules.

Cheraser had a new love for people, but this carried a certain amount of anguish, as he started to notice the needs of others and the pain in their lives. It seemed it would be a massive task to share his faith in the right way, but he remembered that when Jesus walked upon the earth, He invested a lot of time into a limited number of people, and His ministry was always rooted in a deep, intimate relationship with God.

Cheraser had started to spend more time with his spiritual Father, talking to Him and reading the Bible, even if sometimes he really didn't feel like doing so. He noticed that he had started to enjoy serving and helping others. Serving was often an act of the will, but it was becoming more and more enjoyable. Of course, there were occasions when he felt like putting himself first, but God was revealing more of His character to him, and changing Cheraser into the likeness of that character.

> As he stepped onto the pathway he made quick progress along it, although his surroundings soon became dry and barren. The journey had turned into a monotonous, tedious trek. But as Cheraser was without opposition at the moment, he made every effort to keep moving forwards.

Cheraser felt his Christian faith was now unshakeable, and as a result of that he had become complacent. His time spent talking and listening to his Father began to decrease, and he started to rely on his own human effort to live a godly life.

Gradually he was moving away from relationship with his creator, and he found it difficult to spend any time in His presence. He started to become bored with reading the Bible, and he began to feel that his Father was always silent. His own peace seemed to have been snatched away, and his love for God and others was slowly being eroded. He wanted some more excitement in his life.

> Cheraser continued his mundane journey. There were no distractions along the way, and no one was giving advice; there was nothing very exciting happening at all. As he progressed, the pathway slowly turned to soft sand. As far as he could see, there was just desert for companionship. Cheraser cried out to his Father, but there was no reply. He felt abandoned by God, and he stopped trying to communicate with Him.
>
> 'Why don't you stop here and refresh yourself,' said a familiar voice.
>
> As Cheraser looked to the side of the sandy path, Stul was lying there, leaning towards him with one hand under her chin. Her attractiveness immediately ended the boredom and loneliness that Cheraser had been feeling.

'I think you need some excitement,' she said, and a seductive smile illuminated her beautiful face.

Cheraser spotted the wooden cross beside her, and the chain around the door of it was unlocked. His heart started to pump with excitement, he stepped quickly through the doorway and he was immersed in immediate exhilaration.

In front of him was a single wooden sign with the word 'Freedom' carved onto it, which pointed to a wide pathway that sloped downwards. He moved forward and ran onto the path, almost falling as the steep slope increased his speed to such an extent that he was barely able to keep his balance. He encountered many wooden crosses, all of which had the chains to their doors unlocked. He enjoyed the sensual delights offered through each doorway, but he only seemed to be satisfied for a short time before he needed to find another cross.

As he ran further down the slope, he realised that behind him, someone was pursuing him relentlessly. The sound of thumping footsteps was always present, and their unremitting noise prevented Cheraser from completely enjoying the journey he was now on. But he refused to look behind to see who those powerful feet belonged to. A gentle voice would occasionally call out, asking him to stop and turn back, but Cheraser was determined to find his way through the entanglement of crosses and discover the excitement and peace he was looking for.

Along the way, Cheraser encountered many people who encouraged him to keep moving forward, urged him not to look back and convinced him that he would soon find eternal happiness. This put his mind at rest as the pathway was becoming colder and darker, almost like twilight in winter.

As he turned a corner of the ever-twisting and confusing pathway, a familiar face appeared. Lutocc had been absent for quite some time, but he was back now, smiling affectionately. He was holding a thick, warm coat, and Cheraser gratefully took it from him and put it on. Lutocc wrapped his arms around his old friend, and then looked back along the path where Cheraser had come from.

> 'Cheraser, you must not look back,' said Lutocc. 'There is someone following you who would like to spoil your fun and take away all your excitement. Just keep walking with me, and I'll protect you, and eventually I will give you complete satisfaction,' he added with an enticing tone.
>
> Lutocc looked at the pursuer with a sly smile, and he uttered something in a language that was unintelligible to Cheraser. As they continued along the pathway, the footsteps of the pursuer became louder, and He called out to Cheraser.
>
> 'Please turn around, and I will rescue you from this path. My plans are to prosper you, not to harm you,' He said, in a compassionate tone.[1]
>
> 'Remember the height from which you have fallen. Change your ways and do the things you did at first.'[2]
>
> Cheraser looked at Lutocc and carried on walking with him. In the distance, he could now hear weeping from the pursuer. The sound of His voice was getting quieter, and the noise from His heavy footsteps was receding.

Cheraser had again started to look at Internet pornography, and he was addicted to viewing it. He had also resumed his interest in the occult. Every time he felt hurt or down, he chose these areas for comfort, with the hope of finding peace. Online pornography was a particularly soothing companion, and he escaped into that fantasy world on an escalating level as he tried to numb the pain of reality. He had pangs of guilt at first, but these soon became less frequent as he embraced counterfeit relationships. He thought that maybe at some point these one-sided associations would satisfy his longing for validation and intimacy, but at the moment they were just making him feel extremely lonely. The God-shaped box within Cheraser had been unlocked when he first made the decision to be in a right relationship with his Creator, and it was filled with something true and good. But now he was trying again to find a key that opened that same box by using his own human strength to try and find satisfaction. His striving resulted in frustration and emptiness, as the lid of the box was buried under an increasing hail of counterfeit spiritual experiences.

---

1 Based on Jeremiah 29:11, the Bible.

2 Based on Revelation 2:5, the Bible.

Cheraser tried to ignore the voice of God, which stopped him from fully enjoying the wrong things he was doing, and eventually he turned all thoughts of his Father off as quickly as he turned the computer on. There was a dark oppression over him, but to try to ease this feeling, he immersed himself in the very things that were causing it.

Cheraser felt uncomfortable around other Christians now, but he thought that he had managed to convince them that his life was all in order. He said the right things and generally bluffed his way through any contact with them, helped by a Christian facade and an insincere smile.

However, Trenom had seen that something was not right. He confronted Cheraser in a gentle and non-judgemental way. Cheraser didn't want to talk, but he soon found his emotions crumbling. He felt guilt and shame, and he couldn't look Trenom in the eye as he poured out the story of the sins he had become involved in. He felt that his mate was about to see him as some kind of New Age pervert.

There was silence for a moment, and then Trenom said something that changed everything.

'I have had a similar struggle with pornography and still battle with temptation', he said. 'Sometimes, when people are determined to ignore God, He lets them become so miserable that eventually they realise how much they want and need Him,' he added.

'I am miserable with this habit, but it feels as if there is no escape from it,' said Cheraser.

'This area of weakness is incredibly difficult to overcome alone, and you will need people to pray for you and support you,' said Trenom sympathetically.

It wasn't so much that Cheraser needed to be accountable to someone, but rather, he had to have people who he could fight the battle with. Of course, for a Christian, the only real way change could be brought about was by the work of the Holy Spirit, but the help of others had been an important part of Trenom's healing. He offered to stand shoulder to shoulder with Cheraser in his fight against this spiritual bondage, and they prayed together.

> Cheraser knelt down on the pathway, consumed with guilt and shame. Lutocc called out to a nearby helper, and almost immediately, Stul also joined them. They tried to persuade him to continue the journey by promising that he was near to finding happiness.

'This pathway leads to a final door that opens the way to an eternal party, and then you will have complete freedom to indulge in anything you want to,' said Lutocc.

'Come on, let's keep going,' added Stul in her usual enticing way.

But Cheraser cried out to his Father and asked Him to come and rescue him.

'Shut up,' said Stul, angrily. 'You will never be forgiven; you have gone too far this time.'

'You will not be able to carry the weight of your shame and guilt away from this pathway,' said Lutocc, in a desperate plea to keep Cheraser moving along.

The pathway began to light up, and Stul and Lutocc frantically tried to find an area of darkness. As Cheraser caught a glimpse of them in the light, they seemed to have retained their attractiveness, but his spirit now discerned pure evil. He had been deceived, and this was not the pathway he should be on. He pleaded with God for forgiveness and asked for his relationship with Him to be restored. The cross that had once contained God's Son came crashing down, and he heard the loud steps of his pursuer again.

Cheraser's heart was full of sorrow, and he couldn't move towards the pursuer because of his guilt and shame. Soon though, the hands of the relentless chaser scooped him up. He still couldn't see Him fully, but he knew it was his Father God.

'I thought that you had stopped pursuing me,' said Cheraser, with heaviness in his heart.

'I would never stop, but you couldn't hear me anymore, and I had to let you go in the direction that you wanted to,' replied the Father. 'I will carry you back to the right pathway, but firstly I need to show you where the crosses on this one actually lead to.'

Cheraser now had a view of this counterfeit path from above. He was in the arms of his Father, protected from the dangers, but he could see every detail as they progressed along the winding route. There were many signposts stating that happiness and satisfaction were nearby.

Cheraser saw millions of people walking on this track who had entered through a multitude of crosses. Some people seemed excited and expectant, but as Cheraser and his Father journeyed further along the path, there seemed to be a gradually increasing atmosphere of sadness. There was a sense of being lost and dissatisfied, as the offer of finding fulfilment still evaded everyone on this pathway. From his new vantage point, Cheraser could see a bewildering entanglement of directions. People ran through a door of one cross and then back out again to find another. Some were crushed in the frenzy of rushing around trying to find peace and happiness, which seemed to be just out of reach. The myriad of twisted parts of the pathway resembled a ball of string that was so tangled up, it was impossible to unravel. It looked as if a high proportion of the human race was in a maze, with the exit cruelly covered up. Some people did seem to be enjoying themselves, but Cheraser could sense that none of them, whatever their state of happiness, were actually going to find what they were looking for on this pathway.

Tiny droplets of water were now falling onto Cheraser, and this was soon accompanied by a quiet sobbing from his Father. God was calling out to everyone on the path, with a loving, powerful voice, but most people didn't pause from their frenetic efforts.

There was still hope for them at the moment, though, and in some areas a gentle breeze blew, and the cross that contained the Son came crashing down. Individuals and some large groups of people accepted the opportunity to be rescued by God and moved onto the narrow pathway, but others had varying attitudes to the cross. Some people shouted abuse at it, some just ignored it and others just gazed quizzically at it, as if they needed time to reflect. It seemed strange to Cheraser that certain people appeared to understand what the cross was all about but still wanted to remain in this seemingly endless maze.

Cheraser's Father continued to carry him, and eventually they reached a large wooden cross with a doorway, the inevitable exit from this pathway for all who stayed on it until the end. The door was covered in beautiful jewellery, and it had an unlocked chain hanging from it. Signs nailed to the cross promised a place of rest and happiness to those that entered. It was situated in a secluded place, separate from the confused mass of the twisted pathway, and there was a din of noise in the distance from the many travellers heading towards it. Every few seconds someone stumbled upon the exit, and then disappeared through the doorway in an instant. There was a majority of old people but a number of younger ones too. Some seemed happy and excited to be here, whilst others were anguished and confused and had found the exit suddenly, without wanting to.

Cheraser felt the arms of his Father tighten around him, and then the door of the cross opened very slightly. They moved closer to view what was inside, and Cheraser immediately let out a piercing scream and vomited violently. What he saw was unimaginable and indescribable but a reality. The wages for being on this pathway were being handed out to those who had just entered, and they were now in a place that was completely separated from God. As the door was closed, Cheraser's mind couldn't comprehend the terror of what he had just seen. His brain couldn't put into rational thought any of the images he had witnessed, but maybe that was a blessing. He cried with His Father, and their hearts beat almost as one.

As Cheraser and Trenom continued to pray, Cheraser began to realise the serious consequences of living life without God. He knew that his Father was a God of compassion and of forgiveness, but also of justice.

God had done everything possible to deal with the effects of His creation's rebellion against Him. There was nothing any person could do to restore his or her broken relationship with God, so He had lovingly sorted it out Himself.

But if people insist on going their own way and not accepting God's offer of forgiveness, then there is nothing left to save them.

Cheraser knew that he had been ignoring the voice of God, and his heart was sorrowful. He had though now been pardoned completely. As he had received undeserved favour from His Father, he now wanted to please Him—not to try and earn God's love, but because of it.

Cheraser was again standing on the pathway, and by his feet were broken pieces of a heart.

'This is your heart, Cheraser. I am going to give you a new one and fulfil my purposes through you,' said God, in a tender voice.[1]

His Father held him tightly, and He started to carry Cheraser away from the counterfeit pathway. Cheraser closed his eyes and snuggled into God's chest. He could hear heavy footsteps racing along, and he could feel compassionate tears falling onto his head. God had rescued him, and His heart delighted in Cheraser. God had missed his friendship so much, and He had longed to restore the relationship with His precious child.

When they reached the pathway that leads to truth and life, God gently lowered Cheraser and then dropped something onto the ground. A gentle breeze rolled it towards Cheraser. It was the lead seal, which brought some timely encouragement. It still read, 'God's possession. Eternal life guaranteed'.[2]

'I was chasing after you to give you this. You dropped it, but it still remained truth,' said God.

Cheraser picked it up and held it tightly. He needed it for when things got tough, as they inevitably would. It assured him that there was a promise of something glorious and lasting at the end of this hard trek.

---

1 Based on Ezekiel 36:26, the Bible.

2 Based on Ephesians 1:13–14, the Bible.

13.

Confronting Strongholds

As Cheraser restarted his journey on the narrow pathway, he immediately felt an arm come across him, and the way ahead was blocked. He couldn't see the person fully, but he could feel the unmistakable heartbeat and breath of his Father. He wondered why God was holding him back on the pathway to life, and he tried to release himself so that he could move on. Cheraser pushed and wrestled and frantically tried to break free. Dripping with sweat and sick with exhaustion, he eventually stopped fighting.

His Father effortlessly carried Cheraser's limp body to a recess at the side of the pathway. Inside was a tree, sheltered in the corner. A gentle wind blew, and it was just strong enough to pull some juicy fruit from the tree's branches. Cheraser, desperately thirsty and hungry, cried out for some of this tender produce. God gathered an abundance of it and fed him until his strength was restored.

Cheraser rose to his feet, still aching from his recent grappling, and he headed towards a plain wooden box that his Father was pointing to. Inside the box was a collection of armour. It looked as though whoever would wear it was going to be involved in a tough battle. There was a sword, shield, helmet, breastplate, belt and a pair of shoes.[1]

God unpacked the box, and Cheraser's heart sank as he was handed the armour. He knew that the journey ahead was going to be hard, and he didn't know if he could handle it.

'I will be with you always,' said the Father reassuringly.[2]

---

1 Based on Ephesians 6:10–17, the Bible.

2 Based on Matthew 28:20, the Bible.

> Cheraser put the armour on, and with the sword at his side, he headed back to the pathway and noticed that he was high on a mountaintop looking down at the glories of creation. Clean, fresh air filled his lungs, and various animal noises blended into a medley of natural music. He didn't ever want to move from this vantage point, but he knew that he must continue his journey.

Cheraser and Trenom spent many hours praying together through their areas of weakness. They had agreed to contact each other at any time if either of them felt in danger of succumbing to temptation. The nature of this temptation meant it could often be late at night. They immersed themselves in God's word and developed a strategy for living away from everything that harmed their relationship with God.

Cheraser also received help from people who were experienced in healing ministry. He needed to be very careful, but with the support of his church minister and trusted Christian friends, he was making progress.

The process of renewing his mind and being changed into the likeness of God's character was beginning, but Cheraser did struggle to shake off old habits. He had come to realise that he could not fight them in his own strength. He needed God to break through strongholds in the spiritual realm, but he also needed to be disciplined himself and continually choose to walk in freedom. For a long time this was incredibly difficult. Cheraser's mind had been filled over the years with many wrong ways of thinking that led to wrong ways of living, and this behaviour pattern was now engraved upon his being. Often, wrong thought processes and actions were his in-built protection to try and shield himself from pain in his life. When God had begun to remove this source of pain relief, it hurt Cheraser so much that it felt like a period of grieving. He craved the false friendship he had found through pornography, and he became irritable and aggressive. He also had physical symptoms, including headaches and nausea. He had fallen so many times into the sin-confess-sin cycle that he had reached a point of being totally miserable. He knew he had to stop this damaging habit, but sometimes it was incredibly hard to resist.

Throughout this season of mental and physical anguish, Cheraser's peace had amazingly returned, his love for other people was growing warm again and he wanted to discover more of God's purposes for his life. He knew he could have nothing more to do with the occult or with the wrong use of sexuality. He just wished that there was a switch within him that God could turn off, so that he would never again want to be involved in activities that spoilt their relationship.

Cheraser slowly surveyed the scenery around him, so that the continuation of his journey would be delayed as long as possible. He reluctantly started to walk again. He was now ready for battle—not looking for a fight, but mentally prepared if an opponent should try to deceive him into leaving this pathway.

Soon enough the way ahead sloped downwards and turned quickly into a sand-filled, barren track. Just ahead were crosses that led to areas of weakness in Cheraser's life. These crosses still contained doors that had unlocked chains, and it appeared easy to enter through them. Before Cheraser had a relationship with God, these doors were wrapped in locked chains that had to be opened by a keyholder, but it appeared it was easier to enter them now. It didn't make sense. He had previously asked God about why this was so, but He had been silent on the issue. Cheraser once again cried out to his Father, asking Him to lock the chains. He wanted nothing more to do with them, and he was frustrated at God's apparent unwillingness to act.

A gentle breeze started to stir, and the voice of God surprised Cheraser.

'Cheraser, sometimes my ways are impossible for you to understand, and you need to trust me. But I will now reveal to you what has happened with these crosses,' said God. 'The chains were unlocked by the keyholders and then locked again after you entered each doorway. They held you captive, and you were a slave to each counterfeit cross. When they gave you keys and told you that you were in control, this was a deception. They always locked you inside to hinder your search for truth,' explained God. 'When you asked for my forgiveness, which I was delighted to lavish upon you, the death and resurrection of my Son unlocked all the chains that held you in spiritual captivity and broke the power of the keyholders,' said God gently.

'But why am I still able to enter the doorways to these crosses,' asked Cheraser, reverent but still curious.

'I didn't create you to be a robot. I have given you freedom to make choices in your life. You can choose life or death, and I say to you now, choose life,' said God, providing a powerful revelation that Cheraser now understood.[1]

As Cheraser came close to one of the crosses, he noticed that Stul was seated next to it. She was bound with chains, but she could talk, and her attractiveness was magnetic.

'Cheraser, the door to my cross is still open. Why don't you just come inside for a short rest,' she said as her seductive eyes widened. Cheraser held up his shield, and with a powerful swing of his sword, silenced her before continuing his journey. He began to run along, far away from her, but conditions were difficult. His feet felt heavy in the sand, and his armour slowed him down. He pondered whether to take it off, but then, as he turned a corner, the sand-filled part of the track came to a sudden end.

The pathway turned to hard mud that was easier to walk upon, but as Cheraser gazed at the sky, thick black clouds gathered. Small droplets of rain soon began to fall, and almost immediately, a ferocious wind dragged ever-increasing amounts of water from the clouds, resulting in a severe storm. The mud path quickly turned into a quagmire that hindered his journey once again. Cheraser felt vulnerable and lonely, and he walked with his head bowed into the heart of the storm.

A familiar voice startled him and made him look up.

'Why don't you come and find knowledge through the doorway to my cross,' said Lutocc. 'The pathway that you are now on is hard work, and there is no excitement. Come and experience power with me.'

Lutocc was seated and bound in chains, but he still sounded convincing. Cheraser was then hit on the helmet by several unknown objects, and he became fearful and

---

1 Based on Deuteronomy 30:19–20.

insecure. Maybe the door to Lutocc's cross would offer some respite from this attack.

'Cheraser, Lutocc's helpers are throwing the objects at you. They are trying to cause confusion and make it easier for Lutocc to persuade you. It is a false promise of security. Hold up your shield, swing your sword, do not take any of your armour off and continue the journey,' said the voice of God.

This revelation gave Cheraser insight, and he chose to stay on the pathway to life. His swinging sword was enough to silence Lutocc, and Cheraser then ran away from him.

The journey was becoming increasingly more difficult to carry on with, as the storm was relentless, and clumps of heavy mud were added to Cheraser's shoes. His armour had equipped him to withstand some strong opposition, but he felt that it was now weighing him down too much. He sat down in the mud and lifted his arm to begin removing his protection. As he did so, he realised he was still holding the lead seal, which reassured him that he would eventually reach his final destination. He had an immediate inner conviction that his armour was essential, and so, despite the storm and his own feelings of exhaustion, Cheraser kept all of his protection in place and decided to press on.

He peeled off clumps of sticky mud from his shoes and was able to struggle into a standing position. However, as Cheraser made an effort to start walking again, he realised that he just didn't have the energy. He fell to his knees, pounded the mud aggressively, and screamed in desperation. There were no audible words, but Cheraser was pleading for his Father's assistance. He knew that his Father was a mighty God who knew him personally. Cheraser didn't always need words to communicate with Him; he just needed a heart that was desperate to know God intimately and trust Him completely through the storms and battles on the pathway to life.

As Cheraser continued to shout and scream, he felt a gentle hand push him forwards. Immediately, he felt secure and safe, and he leant back into the comforting protection of his Father.

He was still surrounded by a raging storm, and opposition was a constant, unwanted travelling companion, but at the moment he was content despite his circumstances.

Stul and Lutocc appeared frequently, and as Cheraser gazed from his Father's protective hand, he could see that they were talking to him, but their words were muffled and their allure was dimmed.

The strength of his Father carrying him made it possible for him to keep making progress.

14.

Created for Purpose

Cheraser relaxed in his Father's hand, almost asleep.

Suddenly, he was gently lowered to the ground. The storm had stopped, the clouds had cleared and Cheraser was surrounded by springs of water. He now realised just how thirsty he had become, and his bone-dry tongue brushed against the coarse roof of his mouth. He collapsed onto his knees, and with his head tilted back, he tasted the cool, life-giving water. The first few gulps made him cough and splutter. The fresh water settled in his stomach with an immediate cold surge, and he drank with desperation to satisfy his craving.

Once refreshed, he splashed water onto his face and sat and gazed at multiple mini-rainbows and stared in wonder at the pathway ahead. It was a lush, green carpet of grass, surrounded by an array of vivid plants with fruit. The unmistakeable voice of His Father called out to him in an adventurous and almost playful voice.

'Cheraser, come and find me. I have some secrets to share with you,' He said, gently.

Cheraser couldn't see his Father, but he was desperate to search for Him, and he was ready to begin the next stage of the journey. With his armour in place and the lead seal in his grasp, he moved past the remaining springs, which sprinkled water gently onto him. He set his feet upon the grassy pathway and soon came to a wooden sign that had the words 'My purpose for you' carved deeply into it. A small arrow on the sign pointed to a recess at the side of the path, and Cheraser headed towards it with excitement.

He tried to gain entry to the recess, but a locked door blocked his way. The sound of footsteps approaching from behind meant that hopefully someone with a key would soon arrive to let him in. He couldn't yet see anyone though, and frustration and impatience began to build up within him. The footsteps remained constant, but this person was travelling at their own unhurried pace and remained out of sight.

Cheraser decided it was time to try to force his way into the recess. He pushed and kicked at the door without any success and tried to find another entrance, but there was no possible way. It needed to be unlocked, but Cheraser didn't really want to hang around much longer. He considered moving back onto the pathway and continuing his journey, but he knew that if he did, he might miss out on something special. He decided that he would wait, as the gradually increasing sound of footsteps surely meant that help was nearby.

As he waited, he could now hear a second set of footsteps approaching. They seemed to be faster and coming from a person that was frantically trying to reach the recess. Cheraser could soon hear the sound of breathlessness, and he was grateful that someone appeared to be making a real effort to reach him quickly. This person had obviously overtaken the owner of the slow set of footsteps, and Cheraser awaited the person's imminent arrival. He was sure that this would be someone to help him, but as he stood with eager hope, he was hit on the helmet by some unknown objects. He quickly looked at his lead seal to reassure himself of his eternal promise, held up his shield and wielded his sword.

After a moment of panic and confusion, Cheraser was in a battle with Aref, who he now realised was a fierce enemy. The attack took Cheraser by surprise, but he was now equipped with the protective armour needed to defeat him. A long and tiring fight ensued, but Aref eventually fled from the scene, leaving Cheraser gasping for breath.

The original footsteps were still audible, but they were moving at the same slow pace. Cheraser put his head into his hands, desperately waiting for someone to let him into the recess.

Eventually, the sound of the footsteps stopped, and before Cheraser could look up, an arm wrapped around him. All he could see was a massive hand unlocking the door to the recess. The unmistakeable noise of his Father's heartbeat surrounded Cheraser, and his own heart seemed to beat in response to that of his creator, giving him strength and life.

As God removed the key from the door, Cheraser caught a glimpse of his Father's palm. Cheraser's name was written on it, and he experienced a sense of love, security and belonging that was indescribable. He knew at that moment that he had been created to worship, love and serve his Father God and to be loved and cherished by Him. For a fleeting moment, everything about life seemed to make sense.

God pushed open the door to the recess, and Cheraser excitedly walked inside. He stared ahead, wide-eyed, as immediately in front of him was an abundance of fruit hanging from numerous small trees. A gentle wind soon pulled a selection of produce to the ground, allowing the branches to swing back higher into the air. Cheraser picked up a substantial amount of fruit and ate it. His intense hunger was quickly satisfied.

After eating, he saw that there was another alcove within this recess. Its door was slightly ajar, and the gentle wind was tenderly blowing it open and closed repeatedly, creating a desire in Cheraser to see what was inside. He cautiously entered, and laid out before him on a bare wooden table was a single book. The book looked plain, and from the outside it didn't appear to be a particularly interesting read. The only words inscribed on the cover were 'Plans and Purposes'.

As Cheraser started to read the first few pages, he was soon aware of the sound of footsteps approaching. As he turned away from the book and looked up, he was startled, as the hands of God wrapped around him tightly, and he was greeted by his creator's joyous laughter. He could hear and feel the heartbeat of his Father again, and they began to read the book together.

Cheraser didn't want to half-heartedly go through the motions of being a Christian. He had seen some people treat Christianity as just another hobby or interest, like sport or shopping, and he didn't want to be like that.

He knew that if he wanted to be an effective child of God, he needed to protect and nurture his relationship with his Father. This meant spending time worshipping and learning with other Christians, but it also meant developing a deep and private relationship with his creator. This was costly in terms of time and sometimes meant that he had to turn off the television, radio, computer or even his mobile phone, but there was no other way. It was all or nothing. If God was who He said He was, then Cheraser wanted Him to be at the centre of everything he did. He was determined to search for the heart of God, so that he could understand more of His character and begin to discover the purposes for which God had created him.

God had made this relationship possible through an incredible act of mercy, and from this intimate friendship, Cheraser knew that loving service to his spiritual Father would inevitably follow.

Cheraser was not famous, and he didn't think that he had much to offer in the way of gifts or personality. He was, in fact, mostly unnoticeable in any group of people, but he was desperate to know the deep things of God and to know and serve Him with all his being, despite his own weaknesses. He wanted to be a part of bringing God's kingdom into this world. With God's help, he wanted to share the gospel message in ways that were appropriate, understandable and authentic to those around him.

Cheraser had heard many Christians speak great spiritual truths, but their behaviour often didn't match the words which they spoke, and so they could not be taken seriously. Cheraser was determined that his words would be backed up by godly actions, but of course, when he did inevitably fail at times, he knew that his Father would drench him in grace.

Cheraser's hunger to know God's purposes for his life was admirable, but his intense search became almost unbearable, and he eventually became impatient. This led to him flitting about in education, jobs and church activities.

There was no doubting Cheraser's enthusiasm, but firstly he needed to be equipped by God, and then released into the correct area of service by his creator at the appointed time. He didn't think he had received a specific calling in any area of his life, and the leadership of Revelation Church advised him to be patient and to keep intimacy and relationship with God as the priority. They also encouraged him to withdraw from most church activities for a period of time, so that he could hear the voice of his Father. They prayed with him and for him, for godly direction.

This caused raised eyebrows from some other Christians who thought Cheraser was losing his faith or just lazy. Those driven by busyness just didn't understand, and sadly, they rarely heard the voice of God, as it was drowned out by the constant clattering of activity. Cheraser had to learn to say no, and he stood firm with the constant support of his church leaders.

Eventually, after a long period of uncertainty, it seemed as if God was beginning to reveal some of His plans and purposes for Cheraser's life, with a gracious offer of service. Cheraser had limited his involvement with church activities, but he had continued to play for the church football team. One evening, after training, Trenom asked him if he would like to take on some responsibility for leadership of the club. The opportunity to serve God in an area where he had a natural interest seemed perfect. However, before he accepted, he felt that he needed to spend time with his creator to find out if this was His will.

As he spent time praying and reading the Bible, Cheraser felt an inner call to become part of the leadership of the football team, but almost immediately he was overwhelmed by fearful thoughts. Was he good enough? What would people think of him? Would the responsibility spoil his enjoyment of playing football?

Cheraser prayed and talked about his concerns with Trenom. He decided to join the leadership team, despite his fears, as there appeared to be a calling from God.

God closed the book and positioned it in the centre of the wooden table. He then held Cheraser's hand, led him out of the alcove, and sat him down near one of the small trees. He gathered some fruit and gently fed Cheraser. They rested for a while and chatted.

Eventually, God pushed the door of the recess open, and asked Cheraser to walk through it. It was time to resume the journey. God told Cheraser to keep his armour on and to look at the lead seal regularly, to remind him of his eternal future. As Cheraser took some deep breaths, his creator started to run along the path. He challenged Cheraser to pursue Him, as He went into the distance. Cheraser stood still, temporarily paralysed by the fearful thought that his Father was leaving him. God knew and understood Cheraser's thoughts and fears completely, and He shouted out a comforting promise.

'I will never leave you, and I will never take away my support or friendship from you. I am leading you into the next part of your journey.'[1]

Cheraser felt afraid, but he decided to continue on his journey despite his feelings, and he ran along the pathway of lush grass. He eventually reached a large wooden door, which was set into a stone wall that stretched across the path and blocked the way ahead.

Cheraser was frustrated at this obstacle, as he thought this would mean another delay. How long would he have to wait this time for someone to come along and help him gain entry?

He sighed with disappointment and leant gently on the door. Amazingly, although it seemed to be of great weight, it started to open. It hadn't needed a great deal of human strength, and it felt like someone had started to pull it open from the other side.

Cheraser moved slowly through the doorway, and he immediately noticed a sign that said 'Your future is this way.' He held his sword tightly and cautiously walked forwards.

Cheraser had a massive desire to help others who were searching for truth on the spiritual journey, and he wanted to be an example of God's love to them. He was particularly keen to get alongside those who didn't fit into the traditional church mould. He had been helped so much by the laid-back and non-threatening Christians at Revelation Football Club. They had been crucial in helping him discover absolute truth, with a non-judgemental but uncompromising example of faith.

For a while now, Cheraser had been thinking and praying about his friends. He had been asking God if he should invite any of them to join the football club. His good mate named Kreese, a nightclub doorman, had come to mind frequently during these prayer times. It was odd because this was the last person that Cheraser felt like asking.

---

1 Based on Deuteronomy 31:8, the Bible.

Kreese had played football in the past, although he was now a bit overweight, but Cheraser didn't think it would do his reputation any good if he played for a church team.

However, at the first opportunity, he tentatively broached the subject.

'I was just wondering if you were interested in playing football?' said Cheraser.

'I have been thinking of starting to play again, but most of my friends are involved in Sunday morning teams,' replied Kreese. 'I never get out of bed before midday,' he added with a smile.

'We play most of our games on a Saturday afternoon,' said Cheraser.

Kreese smiled again and said, 'That would be ideal, but I know you play for a church team and I don't want to go to church.'

'The team isn't about getting numbers into church. You can just play football. How about you come along to training?' asked Cheraser.

Kreese just nodded slightly, with an expression on his face that indicated he was interested, but a little wary. He had never taunted Cheraser about his faith. He seemed to have respect for the way Cheraser had changed as a person, and he realised that something or someone had made a dramatic difference to his life.

Kreese started to attend training and continued to turn up faithfully every week, eventually gaining a place in the team. He was quiet and unemotional, but he seemed to be watching everything that went on very closely. He also started to attend some of the club social events and relaxed a bit more around the other players. He began to ask the occasional question about spirituality, although he was quick to change the subject when he had heard enough.

Cheraser sometimes felt a bit embarrassed when talking about spiritual matters with Kreese. He was a lovely guy, but Cheraser saw him as tough and uncompromising and didn't think he would be that interested in God.

He soon realized that was a wrong thought pattern though. Kreese may not have been interested in coffee mornings, old-fashioned church services or bad drama, but God desperately wanted to restore a relationship with him. He had plans for him which were full of adventure, and they wouldn't crush the passion for life that he had.

Cheraser often felt inadequate as a Christian, especially in his leadership role with Revelation Football Club. The leadership team met up regularly, and they prayed faithfully for the continued vision of the club and for individual players like Kreese. But no new believers had emerged recently.

This was something that Cheraser took personally, and he had to keep reminding himself that he couldn't convert people; only the power of God could do that. He also felt guilty because he wasn't always a good example of a Christian, but he continued with the help of God's power and grace to fight against the weaknesses in his own life.

God had called him to serve within this football team, and by faith he persevered, trusting that God would fulfil His own purposes.

> Cheraser was making slow progress on the pathway, and he had had many energy sapping encounters with Stul, Lutocc and Aref. He had been trudging along the grass for a long time, and he barely noticed the beauty of creation surrounding him. He was frustrated and weary. He stopped, fell to his knees and took some long breaths of air. As he paused, he once again recognised the blessings that were all around. There were springs of water and delicious-looking fruit nearby, which would sustain him on his journey, if only he would take the time to eat and drink.
>
> As Cheraser realised that he must re-fuel his body, he ate and drank, and then became aware of his Father's presence. He felt a gentle nudge towards the edge of the pathway, and he soon discovered another recess hidden behind a cluster of fruit trees. He walked through an open doorway, and he immediately saw the football leadership team entering the recess, simultaneously, through separate doorways. Everyone sat around a wooden table that had Kreese's name engraved in the middle, and each person prayed that God would reveal Himself to Kreese.
>
> After a while, Cheraser flared his nostrils and inhaled beautiful-smelling incense. He opened his eyes to see smoke rising from a golden bowl in the middle of the table. As he looked upwards, Cheraser could see the hands of God gently wafting the aroma towards Himself.[1]

---

1 Based on Revelation 5:8, the Bible.

As he looked around at his fellow leaders, Cheraser saw that they were visibly ageing, as though this prayer session signified a long period of time. But it also seemed to be somehow outside of time, in a way that Cheraser couldn't quite comprehend.

As the group prayed, unseen action was taking place in the spiritual realm. Fierce battles were being fought, and unknown to Cheraser and his friends, the wooden cross that held the sacrifice of God's Son came crashing down onto the ground in front of Kreese.

Kreese could see that something was nailed to the cross. He gasped as he immediately recognised that it was a human body. The arms of Father God wrapped around Kreese, and He helped him walk around the battered and broken figure that was screaming in agony. The man on the cross looked like He had no strength left, but as Kreese gazed at Him, he could see that He was carrying an incredible weight. Kreese was then violently sick, as a completely vile smell reached his nasal passage.

'This revolting stench is caused by the wrong thoughts, words and actions of every single person that has ever existed,' said God gently. 'My Son is the only person who has ever lived a sinless life. Yet here He is, blameless and pure, nailed to a cross, and carrying the weight of mankind's rebellion against me on His shoulders.'

Kreese continued to look at the tortured man on the cross. When He finally died, a large group of ecstatic figures appeared. They put chains around Him and hurled a ceaseless barrage of vicious insults at the lifeless body. Father God held and comforted Kreese, but for a while He could not look at His own Son. Kreese turned his own eyes away from the cross, and tried to make sense of what he had seen.

Eventually, there was the sound of metal being ripped apart. The Son of God had broken free from the chains that held Him, and He had resurrected from the dead. The figures who had chained Him up and insulted Him were silenced, and they fled, desperately trying to find cover.

An incredible celebration then followed, as Father and Son embraced. Holy, perfect music surrounded them, and

Kreese eventually had to cover his ears, as the realisation of his own separation from God began to dawn on him.

Kreese stood on the wooden frame as it lay on the ground, and he looked at the blood and bits of human flesh that remained upon it. He felt the weight of his own selfishness forcing him onto his knees. He was unable to keep walking.

'Let me take the weight from you. It can be left on the cross forever,' said a gentle voice. 'Then let me carry you over the cross to a new pathway.'

Kreese looked up and saw a wall, just ahead of the cross, which blocked the new path. In the wall was a doorway with a chain wrapped around it. Suddenly there was a mighty crash as the chain fell off.

Kreese stared ahead knowing he had a decision to make. He then looked back at the pathway he had travelled on since he was conceived. It offered many doorways to happiness and fulfilment. He hadn't found true satisfaction during the time he had spent journeying on it, but the surroundings were familiar, and it was still an appealing option.

'You can choose to walk upon the pathway that leads to life or the pathway that leads to death,' said God. 'Now choose life, but you must choose.'[1]

Kreese's decision should have been easy in the eternal scheme of things. But sometimes truth is ignored for many reasons. Whatever Kreese decided, it would one day have consequences.

As Cheraser left the recess, he felt insecure about progressing further along the path. He was tempted to stop his journey and take shelter, to avoid any dangerous situations that he might encounter. As he paused, he remembered the lead seal.[2] He gripped it tightly, and a feeling of encouragement immediately surged through his body. His desire to carry on and pursue the adventurous route, even though the terrain would be rough, had become very strong. He shook with apprehension, stood

---

1 Based on Deuteronomy 30:19–20, the Bible.

2 Based on Ephesians 1:13–14, the Bible.

> with his arms outstretched and pleaded with God to lead him further along this mysterious track. He fell to his knees, exhausted by the intensity of his emotions, and waited in silence.
>
> A playful voice soon brought some relief to Cheraser's high-strung mood. The sound of God's words seemed to bring an atmosphere of calmness and indescribable joy.
>
> 'Cheraser, come and find me. This may be a difficult and lonely journey, but it is a safe and secure path if you keep listening to my direction,' said God in a tender tone.
>
> Something inside Cheraser was ignited, and he delighted in chasing after his creator. God kept calling from secret hidden places ahead, and Cheraser pursued Him with an excited anticipation. The places they ended up together were sometimes tough to reach but always full of unimaginable joy and satisfaction. This was still only the journey though, and, frustratingly, Cheraser could only see God in part. He would have to wait until he arrived at his final destination to see his creator fully. He pressed on towards that glorious hope, always trying to keep a perspective on the fact that one day he would come face to face with his maker, and then they would discuss his whole journey.[1]

Cheraser was now passionately searching for the true character of his creator, and as he encountered more of Him, the power of God began to transform his heart into its originally intended condition. In an eternal sense he was safe and secure, and his heart felt truly alive. He had overcome passivity, and he embraced life as an adventure to be lived with an eternal perspective, focused on the purposes of God.

Most of Cheraser's non-Christian friends thought that being a Christian would mean missing out on life. This was the biggest lie that they could ever believe.

God created the human race to live in a world that was full of mystery and adventure, but within a secure environment which only comes from being in relationship with Him. That relationship was messed up by the people that God had created, and each one tried to find adventure and purpose without Him.

---

1 Based on Philippians 3:14, the Bible.

Therefore, all the keys that they turned in their life would never unlock a door which led to lasting security and satisfaction.

God had used passionate Christians to share His saving plan with Cheraser. They had taken a risk by shaking up the traditional church establishment in a godly way. They had managed to knock some holes in the concrete walls of church culture, and this made the truth more accessible. Cheraser had peered through the jagged holes suspiciously at first, but he had then started a long journey to find the person who held the key to eternal life.

The people that God had worked through had shown Cheraser an authentic faith that was inclusive to all, and the way in which they had communicated the gospel message had sometimes made them unpopular with fellow Christians. But if every Christian chose a comfortable and risk-free journey, then many spiritual searchers would probably never find the key that God turns to unlock absolute truth.

www.ingramcontent.com/pod-product-compliance
Ingram Content Group UK Ltd.
Pitfield, Milton Keynes, MK11 3LW, UK
UKHW041940190726
13854UKWH00004B/1693

9 781447 744238